THE TREES OF
Dehra

Ruskin Bond is known for his signature simplistic and witty writing style. He is the author of several bestselling short stories, novellas, collections, essays and children's books; and has contributed a number of poems and articles to various magazines and anthologies. At the age of twenty-three, he won the prestigious John Llewellyn Rhys Prize for his first novel, *The Room on the Roof*. He was also the recipient of the Padma Shri in 1999, Lifetime Achievement Award by the Delhi Government in 2012, and the Padma Bhushan in 2014.

Born in 1934, Ruskin Bond grew up in Jamnagar, Shimla, New Delhi and Dehradun. Apart from three years in the UK, he has spent all his life in India, and now lives in Landour, Mussoorie, with his adopted family.

THE TREES OF

Dehra

RUSKIN BOND

RUPA

Published by
Rupa Publications India Pvt. Ltd 2020
7/16, Ansari Road, Daryaganj
New Delhi 110002

Sales centres:
Allahabad Bengaluru Chennai
Hyderabad Jaipur Kathmandu
Kolkata Mumbai

Calligraphy by Abhinandan Khanna

ISBN: 978-93-89967-48-7

First impression 2020

10 9 8 7 6 5 4 3 2 1

Printed at HT Media Ltd, Gr. Noida

Contents

Introduction

All trees are friendly, but some trees are friendlier than others.

The mango tree is probably my favourite. The fragrance of mango blossoms welcomed me back to India after a long stay abroad. Its canopy of leaves gave me shade on a summer's day. And its golden fruit has sustained me over the years.

Cherry trees in blossom, apricots, plums, peaches, apples, in fruit or in blossom, bring the Himalayan foothills to life in the early spring.

In the plains, the jamun competes with the mango for my affections. And whenever I see a jackfruit tree, I remember the old jackfruit tree that gave shade to the veranda of my grandmother's bungalow in Dehradun. And a wonderful pickle she made from the generous jackfruit!

Up here in the hills, I can hear the wind humming in the pine trees.

It is still winter, and the chestnut trees are bare. But a few weeks from now, they will be in new leaf, and then in April, those glorious pink and white profusions of blossom will appear.

In Kolkata last week, I saw a wonderful old banyan tree, centuries old. And back home, I found a little orange tree had sprung up from a seed that had found its way into a small flowerpot.

The seed, the stem, the leaves, the flower, the fruit! Can there be a greater miracle?

Ruskin Bond
February, 2020

The Willow

The next time you see your favourite cricket player smashing sixes all over the field, spare a thought for the bat that does the job for him. The best cricket bats are made from the timber of the willow tree.

The willow grows easily in our temperate climate, and you will find it growing beside streams as well as in gardens and roadside avenues. Its leaves and branches droop gracefully to the water's edge. Artists loved to depict the willow in their paintings of romantic landscapes.

It is a graceful tree, bare in winter but one of the first to come into leaf with the onset of spring. Its timber is tough, pliable; it will take a battering from a cricket ball. A broken branch will take root easily in damp earth; so will the falling seeds; which is why the willow flourishes on the banks of ponds or streams.

Artificial limbs are also made from the wood of the willow. A tree that is both useful and attractive; not just the 'weeping willow' of legend.

While on the subject of willow trees, do read Kenneth Grahame's children's classic, *The Wind in the Willows*, a story about riverside life and the small creatures who dwell along the banks of the river.

Music in the Trees

In India, the monsoon is the season when our insect orchestra is at its best. It is true that the shrill music of the cicada is heard throughout the hot weather; but theirs is a prelude to the great concert that comes into full play once the rainy season begins. When the monsoon with its magic touch brings life and greenness to rock and earth and tree, the whole air seems to come alive with the music of insects. Grasshoppers shrill in the bushes, crickets chirp from under stones, and in the water-laden fields there are hundreds of minor artists providing a medley of sounds.

Amongst our more vocal and better-known insect musicians are those that dwell in trees, the cicadas and the crickets. As musicians, the cicadas are in a class by themselves. Most of the species in India are forest dwellers, but there are some who inhabit the open country in the plains. All through the hot weather their chorus rings through the jungle, while a shower of rain, far from damping their spirits, only rouses them to a deafening, combined effort. The ancient Greeks knew the cicada well. They appreciated his music so much that they kept him captive in a cage to sing. Only the males were chosen, for the females, like most insect musicians, were completely dumb. This moved one of the Greek poets to exclaim, 'Happy are the cicadas, for they have voiceless wives.'

The cicada's sound-producing organs are amongst the most remarkable in the animal kingdom. The underside of his body carries a pair of flaps, each of which covers an oval membrane, which looks like the head of a drum. These are set into motion by a great pair of muscles attached to them from within the body, and the sound is produced by their vibration. The whole abdomen, which is practically hollow, helps to increase or diminish the sound.

Simple, isn't it? To be truthful, I find it extremely complicated, and am able to describe the process only by consulting the notes of S.H. Prater, one-time curator of the Bombay Natural History Society.

Let it be added that the female carries these structures in a modified form, but as she has no muscles to bring them into play, she is unable to use them. This is why she must remain silent while her spouse shrieks away. I would change the line from that Greek poet (Xenarchos, I think) and say instead: 'Pity the female cicadas, for they have singing husbands!'

The object of the cicadas' mirthful music is a mystery. It may attract the opposite sex, or it may be just a diversion of the male. Or perhaps he sings because he is happy.

The tree crickets are a band of willing artists who commence their performance as soon as it is dusk. Their sounds are familiar, but the crickets are seldom seen. If one of them enters the house and treats us to a solo, the sound is so surprisingly loud that we can hardly believe it is being produced by so small a creature.

The common Indian tree cricket is a delicate pale-green little creature with hazy, transparent green wings. In full song he holds his wings outspread over his back. They vibrate so rapidly that they are but a blurred outline. A tap on the bush or leaf on which he sits will put an immediate stop to his performance. His music ceases, and he lowers his wings and folds them flat on his back. The grasshopper makes his music by rubbing his legs against his forewing.

I won't go into detail over how the cricket produces its music, except to say that its louder notes are produced by a rapid vibration of the wings, the right wing usually working over the left, and the edge of one acting on the file of the other to produce a shrill, long-sustained note.

One of the best-known crickets is a large black fellow who lives underground and rarely comes out by day, except when the rains flood him out of his burrow. But when night falls, he sits on his doorstep and pours out his soul in a strident song. This cricket's name is as impressive as his sound—*Brachytrypes portentosus.*

The mole cricket is a genius by itself. Mole crickets are tillers of the soil. They use their powerful forelimbs for shovelling up the earth and their hard heads for butting into it. Notwithstanding its earthy occupations, the mole cricket is sometimes moved to creating music. But as he repeats his note—a solemn deep-toned chirp, about a hundred times a minute—the performance can be monotonous.

In India, the cone-headed katydids are probably the most notable performers. Katydids are trim, slender grasshopper-like insects, much in evidence in the fresh green grass of the monsoon. In the fields, the loud, shrill notes of the males may be heard both by day and by night. Sometimes one of them comes into a house and treats its occupants to a sudden outburst of high-pitched fiddling. His song rises in pitch as the performer warms to his work. In a room it can be quite deafening, and the sound is always difficult to locate—it seems to come from everywhere.

Finally we come to the tree crickets, a band of willing artistes who commence their performance at dusk. Their sounds are familiar, but it is difficult to see the musicians. Presumably the males sing in order to attract their more silent females. The music advertises the presence of the male; just as in other creatures, it is the colour or smell that does the job. And if music be the food of love, play on, cicada!

Why are grasshoppers and crickets such persistent little singers? Do they really sing to charm and attract the females, or is their song the voice of mirth? A curious habit has been noticed among certain tree crickets, which may offer a clue to the mystery. Sometimes, as a male sings, a female steals up to him from behind. The male ceases his music. He sits quite still with his wings uplifted. The female noses about his back and soon discovers the object of her search—a deep cavity situated just behind the base of his wings. This cavity contains a clear liquid which she eagerly laps up. Well, even the human male seeks to please his sweetheart with the offer of chocolates.

It is supposed that in this instance, the lady is attracted rather by the sweets the male has to offer than by his music. But the music advertises his whereabouts. She hears his sound and knows that he has a sweet nectar to offer her and comes after it. If the artful luring of the male sometimes results in mating, we see the real reason for the male possessing his musical instruments, and understand his urge to play them so continuously. After all, the luring of the female with music and sweets is even practised by human beings. It may not always succeed in its purpose. Sometimes, as with the crickets, the female accepts the gifts so generously offered—and then takes her leave!

The Trees Are Walking

Koki and her grandmother were sitting on a string cot in the shade of an old jackfruit tree, and Grandmother was talking about her father and his great love for trees and flowers.

Grandmother said, 'I was never able to get over the feeling that plants and trees loved my father with as much tenderness as he loved them. I was sitting beside him on the veranda steps one morning, when I noticed the tendril of a creeping vine that was trailing near my feet. As we sat there in the soft winter sunshine, I saw the tendril moving very slowly away from me and towards my father. Twenty minutes later it had crossed the veranda steps and was touching my father's feet.

'There is probably a scientific explanation for the plant's behaviour—something to do with light and warmth—but I like to think that it moved simply because it was fond of my father.

'One felt like drawing close to him. Sometimes when I sat alone beneath a tree I would feel a little lonely or lost. But as soon as my father joined me, the garden would become a happy place, the tree itself more friendly.

'Your great-grandfather had served many years in the

Indian Forest Service and so it was natural that he should know, understand and like trees. On his retirement he built this bungalow on the outskirts of the town, planting the trees that you see around it now: limes, mangoes, oranges and guavas; also jacaranda and laburnum and the Persian lilac. In our valley, given the chance, plants and trees grow tall and strong.

'Of course there were other trees here before the house was built, including an old peepul which had forced its way through the walls of an old, abandoned temple, knocking the bricks down with its vigorous growth. Peepul trees are great show-offs. Even when there is no breeze, their broad-chested, slim-waisted leaves will spin like tops, determined to attract your attention and invite you into the shade.'

'What happened to the temple?' asked Koki.

'Well, my mother wanted the peepul tree cut down, but my father said he would save both the tree and the temple. So he rebuilt the temple around the tree, and there it is, on the other side of the wall. The tree protects the temple, and the temple protects the tree. People from these parts feel there's a friendly tree spirit dwelling there, and they bring offerings of flowers and leave them at the base of the tree.

'Did you know that I used to climb trees when I was a girl? This jackfruit was my favourite tree, it's quite easy to climb. You climb it too, don't you?

'Another good tree was the banyan behind the house. Its spreading branches, which hung to the ground and took root again, formed a number of twisting passageways. The tree was older than the house, older than my grandparents. I could hide in its branches, behind a screen of thick green leaves, and spy on the world below.

'Yes, the banyan tree was a world in itself, populated with small animals and large insects. While the leaves were still pink and tender, they would be visited by the delicate Map Butterfly, who left her eggs to their care.

'At night the tree was visited by the Hawk-Cuckoo. Its shrill nagging cry kept us awake on hot summer nights. We call the bird 'papiha', which means 'rain is coming!' But, Father said that according to Englishmen living in India, it seemed to be shouting up and up the scale: 'Oh dear, oh dear! How very hot it's getting! We feel it…we feel it…we feel it!'

'Well, the banyan has long since gone. It came down in a storm, aerial roots and all. Father planted another, but, as you can see, it's still quite a young tree. The banyan takes a long time to grow.

'Your great-grandfather wasn't content with planting trees in the garden or near the house. During the monsoons he would walk into the scrubland and beyond the riverbed, armed with cuttings and saplings, and he would plant them out there, hoping to create a forest. But, grazing cattle always finished them off.

'No one ever goes there,' I said. 'Who will see your forest?'

'We are not planting it for people to see,' said my father. 'We are planting it for the earth—and for the birds and animals who live on it and need more food and shelter.'

'Father told me why mankind, and not only wild creatures, need trees—for keeping the desert away, for attracting rain, for preventing the banks of rivers from being washed away. But everywhere people are cutting down trees without planting new ones. If this continues, then one day there will be no forests at all and the world will become one great desert!

'The thought of a world without trees became a sort of nightmare for me. It's one reason why I shall never want to live on a treeless moon! I helped my father in his tree-planting with even greater enthusiasm.

'One day the trees will move again,' he said. 'They have been standing still for thousands of years, but one day they will move again. There was a time when trees could walk about like people. Then, along came a terrible demon and cast a spell over them, rooting them to one place. But they are always trying to move—see how they reach out with their arms!'

'On one of our walks along the river bank about a mile upstream from here, we found an island, a small rocky island in the middle of the riverbed. You know what this riverbed is like—dry during summers but flooded during the monsoons. A young tamarind tree was growing in the middle of the island, and my father said, 'If a tamarind can grow here, so can other trees.'

'As soon as the monsoon arrived—and while the river could still be crossed—we set out with a number of mango, laburnum, hibiscus and coral tree saplings and cuttings, and spent the better part of a day planting them on the little island. We made one more visit to the island before the monsoon finally set in. Most of the plants looked quite healthy.

'The monsoon season is the best time for rambling about. At every turn there is something new to see. Out of earth and rock and leafless bough, the magic touch of the summer rain brings forth new life and verdure. You can almost see the broad-leaved vines growing. Plants spring up in the most unlikely places. A peepul took root on the roof; a, mango sprouted on the windowsill. My father and I did not want to remove them, but they had to go if the house was to be prevented from falling down!

'If you two want to live in a tree, that's all right by me,' said my mother. 'But I like having a roof over my head, and I'm not going to have it brought down by a hanging forest. Already I can see roots breaking in through the ceiling!'

'The visiting trees were carefully removed and transplanted in the garden. Whenever we came indoors from our gardening and sat down to a meal, a ladybird or a caterpillar would invariably walk off our sleeves and wander about the kitchen, much to mother's annoyance.

'There were flowers in the garden, too; my mother loved fragrant flowers, like roses and sweet peas and jasmine and Queen of the Night. But my father and I found trees more exciting. They kept growing and changing and attracting birds and other visitors.

'The banyan tree really came to life during the monsoon. The branches were thick with scarlet figs. We couldn't eat the berries, but the many birds that gathered in the tree—gossipy rosy-pastors, quarrelsome mynas, cheerful bulbuls and coppersmiths, and sometimes a noisy, bullying crow—would feast on them. And when night fell and the birds were resting, the dark flying foxes flapped heavily about the tree, chewing and munching loudly as they clambered over the branches.

'The tree crickets were a band of willing artistes who would start singing at almost any time of the day. At the height of the monsoon, the banyan tree was like an orchestra with the musicians constantly tuning up.

'When I grew up, I was married and went to live with your grandfather in Bombay. We were there for many years, and I could only visit my parents here once or twice in all that time. I had no brothers, so, when my parents died, they left the house to me. It will be yours one day. Would you rather live here or in that poky little house in the town?'

'Here,' said Koki. 'But only if you are here too, Granny.'

'The trees will be here,' said Granny.

'And what about the island?' asked Koki. 'The trees you planted with your father—are they still there?'

'You can see them for yourself if you feel like a walk. But I'll tell you what I found when I came to live here again after twenty years or more. I walked out of the old house and took the same path that my father and I used to take during our walks.

'It was February, I remember, and as I looked across the dry riverbed, my eye was immediately caught by the spectacular red plunges of the coral blossom. In contrast with the dry riverbed, the island was a small green paradise. When I walked over to the trees, I noticed that a number of parrots had come to live in them. A small spotted deer scampered away to hide in a thicket. And a wild pheasant challenged me with a mellow 'Who-are-you, who-are-you?'

'But the trees seemed to know me. I am sure they whispered among themselves and beckoned me nearer.

'I ran my hands over their barks and it was like touching the hands of old friends. And looking around, I noticed that other small trees and wild plants and grasses had sprung up under the protection of those whom we had planted there.

'The trees had multiplied! The forest was on the move! In one small corner of the world, my father's dream was coming true, and trees were walking again!'

Whispering Pines

Well, my favourite pine tree does talk a little, or rather it hums and whispers when the afternoon breeze slips over the mountains.

This is a Chir pine that grows on a rocky outcrop below Pari Tibba, on the hill facing Landour. When I was younger, I would scramble down the hillside, notebook in hand, and write a poem or a short story in the shelter of this fragrant pine. Sometimes words seemed to emanate from the tree. Of course it was just the wind playing tricks on me. But it did give me a few ideas!

The pine is not as tall or as durable as the deodar, but it comes in several varieties—there's the Blue pine and the Khasi pine and the long-leaved Chir pine, and don't forget the Chilgoza pine, which grows at higher altitudes and gives us those delicious and nutritious chilgozas!

The School among the Pines

1

A leopard, lithe and sinewy, drank at the mountain stream, and then lay down on the grass to bask in the late February sunshine. Its tail twitched occasionally and the animal appeared to be sleeping. At the sound of distant voices it raised its head to listen, then stood up and leapt lightly over the boulders in the stream, disappearing among the trees on the opposite bank.

A minute or two later, three children came walking down the forest path. They were a girl and two boys, and they were singing in their local dialect an old song they had learnt from their grandparents.

'Five more miles to go!
We climb through rain and snow.
A river to cross…
A mountain to pass…
Now we've four more miles to go!'

Their school satchels looked new, their clothes had been washed and pressed. Their loud and cheerful singing startled a Spotted Forktail. The bird left its favourite rock in the stream and flew down the dark ravine.

'Well, we have only three more miles to go,' said the bigger boy, Prakash, who had been this way hundreds of times. 'But first we have to cross the stream.'

He was a sturdy twelve-year-old with eyes like raspberries and a mop of bushy hair that refused to settle down on his head. The girl and her younger brother were taking this path for the first time.

'I'm feeling tired, Bina,' said the little boy.

Bina smiled at him, and Prakash said, 'Don't worry, Sonu, you'll get used to the walk. There's plenty of time.' He glanced at the old watch he'd been given by his grandfather. It needed constant winding. 'We can rest here for five or six minutes.'

They sat down on a smooth boulder and watched the clear water of the shallow stream tumbling downhill. Bina examined the old watch on Prakash's wrist. The glass was badly scratched and she could barely make out the figures on the dial. 'Are you sure it still gives the right time?' she asked.

'Well, it loses five minutes every day, so I put it ten minutes forward at night. That means by morning it's quite accurate! Even our teacher, Mr Mani, asks me for the time. If he doesn't ask, I tell him! The clock in our classroom keeps stopping.'

They removed their shoes and let the cold mountain water run over their feet. Bina was the same age as Prakash. She had pink cheeks, soft brown eyes, and hair that was just beginning to lose its natural curls. Hers was a gentle face, but a determined little chin showed that she could be a strong person. Sonu, her younger brother, was ten. He was a thin boy who had been sickly as a child but was now beginning to fill out. Although he did not look very athletic, he could run like the wind.

Bina had been going to school in her own village of Koli, on the other side of the mountain. But it had been a Primary School, finishing at Class Five. Now, in order to study in the Sixth, she would have to walk several miles every day to Nauti, where there was a High School going up to the Eighth. It had been decided that Sonu would also shift to the new school, to give Bina company. Prakash, their neighbour in Koli, was already a pupil at the Nauti school. His mischievous nature, which sometimes got him into trouble, had resulted in his having to repeat a year.

But this didn't seem to bother him. 'What's the hurry?' he had told his indignant parents. 'You're not sending me to a foreign land when I finish school. And our cows aren't running away, are they?'

'You would prefer to look after the cows, wouldn't you?' asked Bina, as they got up to continue their walk.

'Oh, school's all right. Wait till you see old Mr Mani. He always gets our names mixed up, as well as the subjects he's supposed to be teaching. At our last lesson, instead of maths, he gave us a geography lesson!'

'More fun than maths,' said Bina.

'Yes, but there's a new teacher this year. She's very young, they say, just out of college. I wonder what she'll be like.'

Bina walked faster and Sonu had some trouble keeping up with them. She was excited about the new school and the prospect of different surroundings. She had seldom been outside her own village, with its small school and single ration shop. The day's routine never varied—helping her mother in the fields or with household tasks like fetching water from the spring or cutting grass and fodder for the cattle. Her father, who was a soldier, was away for nine months in the year and Sonu was still too small for the heavier tasks.

As they neared Nauti village, they were joined by other children coming from different directions. Even where there were no major roads, the mountains were full of little lanes and shortcuts. Like a game of snakes and ladders, these narrow paths zigzagged around the hills and villages, cutting through fields and crossing narrow ravines until they came together to form a fairly busy road along which mules, cattle and goats joined the throng.

Nauti was a fairly large village, and from here a broader but dustier road started for Tehri. There was a small bus, several trucks and (for part of the way) a road-roller. The road hadn't been completed because the heavy diesel roller couldn't take the steep climb to Nauti. It stood on the roadside halfway up the road from Tehri.

Prakash knew almost everyone in the area, and exchanged greetings and gossip with other children as well as with muleteers, bus drivers, milkmen and labourers working on the road. He loved telling everyone the time, even if they weren't interested.

'It's nine o'clock,' he would announce, glancing at his wrist. 'Isn't your bus leaving today?'

'Off with you!' the bus driver would respond, 'I'll leave when I'm ready.'

As the children approached Nauti, the small flat school buildings came into view on the outskirts of the village, fringed with a line of long-leaved pines. A small crowd had assembled on the playing field. Something unusual seemed to have happened. Prakash ran forward to see what it was all about. Bina and Sonu stood aside, waiting in a patch of sunlight near the boundary wall.

Prakash soon came running back to them. He was bubbling over with excitement.

'It's Mr Mani!' he gasped. 'He's disappeared! People are saying a leopard must have carried him off!'

2

Mr Mani wasn't really old. He was about fifty-five and was expected to retire soon. But for the children, adults over forty seemed ancient! And Mr Mani had always been a bit absent-minded, even as a young man.

He had gone out for his early morning walk, saying he'd be back by eight o'clock, in time to have his breakfast and be ready for class. He wasn't married, but his sister and her husband stayed with him. When it was past nine o'clock his sister presumed he'd stopped at a neighbour's house for breakfast (he loved tucking into other people's breakfast) and that he had gone on to school from there. But when the school bell rang at ten o'clock, and everyone but Mr Mani was present, questions were asked and guesses were made.

No one had seen him return from his walk and enquiries made in the village showed that he had not stopped at anyone's house. For Mr Mani to disappear was puzzling; for him to disappear without his breakfast was extraordinary.

Then a milkman returning from the next village said he had

seen a leopard sitting on a rock on the outskirts of the pine forest. There had been talk of a cattle-killer in the valley, of leopards and other animals being displaced by the construction of a dam. But as yet no one had heard of a leopard attacking a man. Could Mr Mani have been its first victim? Someone found a strip of red cloth entangled in a blackberry bush and went running through the village showing it to everyone. Mr Mani had been known to wear red pyjamas. Surely, he had been seized and eaten! But where were his remains? And why had he been in his pyjamas?

Meanwhile, Bina and Sonu and the rest of the children had followed their teachers into the school playground. Feeling a little lost, Bina looked around for Prakash. She found herself facing a dark slender young woman wearing spectacles, who must have been in her early twenties—just a little too old to be another student. She had a kind, expressive face and she seemed a little concerned by all that had been happening.

Bina noticed that she had lovely hands; it was obvious that the new teacher hadn't milked cows or worked in the fields!

'You must be new here,' said the teacher, smiling at Bina. 'And is this your little brother?'

'Yes, we've come from Koli village. We were at school there.'

'It's a long walk from Koli. You didn't see any leopards, did you? Well, I'm new too. Are you in the Sixth class?'

'Sonu is in the Third. I'm in the Sixth.'

'Then I'm your new teacher. My name is Tania Ramola. Come along, let's see if we can settle down in our classroom.'

Mr Mani turned up at twelve o'clock, wondering what all the fuss was about. No, he snapped, he had not been attacked by a leopard; and yes, he had lost his pyjamas and would someone kindly return them to him?

'How did you lose your pyjamas, Sir?' asked Prakash.

'They were blown off the washing line!' snapped Mr Mani.

After much questioning, Mr Mani admitted that he had gone further than he had intended, and that he had lost his way coming back. He had been a bit upset because the new teacher, a slip of a girl, had been given charge of the Sixth, while he was still with the Fifth, along with that troublesome boy Prakash, who kept on reminding him of the time! The headmaster had explained that as Mr Mani was due to retire at the end of the year, the school did not wish to burden him with a senior class. But Mr Mani looked upon the whole thing as a plot to get rid of him. He glowered at Miss Ramola whenever he passed her. And when she smiled back at him, he looked the other way!

Mr Mani had been getting even more absent-minded of late—putting on his shoes without his socks, wearing his homespun waistcoat inside out, mixing up people's names, and of course, eating other people's lunches and dinners. His sister had made a special mutton broth (pai) for the postmaster, who was down with flu and had asked Mr Mani to take it over in a thermos. When the postmaster opened the thermos, he found only a few drops of broth at the bottom—Mr Mani had drunk the rest somewhere along the way.

When sometimes Mr Mani spoke of his coming retirement, it was to describe his plans for the small field he owned just behind the house. Right now, it was full of potatoes, which did not require much looking after; but he had plans for growing dahlias, roses, French beans, and other fruits and flowers.

The next time he visited Tehri, he promised himself, he would buy some dahlia bulbs and rose cuttings. The monsoon season would be a good time to put them down. And meanwhile, his potatoes were still flourishing.

3

Bina enjoyed her first day at the new school. She felt at ease with Miss Ramola, as did most of the boys and girls in her class. Tania Ramola had been to distant towns such as Delhi and Lucknow—places they had only read about—and it was said that she had a brother who was a pilot and flew planes all over the world. Perhaps he'd fly over Nauti someday!

Most of the children had, of course, seen planes flying overhead, but none of them had seen a ship, and only a few had been on a train. Tehri mountain was far from the railway and hundreds of miles from the sea. But they all knew about the big dam that was being built at Tehri, just forty miles away.

Bina, Sonu and Prakash had company for part of the way home, but gradually the other children went off in different directions. Once they had crossed the stream, they were on their own again.

It was a steep climb all the way back to their village. Prakash had a supply of peanuts which he shared with Bina and Sonu, and at a small spring they quenched their thirst.

When they were less than a mile from home, they met a postman who had finished his round of the villages in the area and was now returning to Nauti.

'Don't waste time along the way,' he told them. 'Try to get home before dark.'

'What's the hurry?' asked Prakash, glancing at his watch. 'It's only five o'clock.'

'There's a leopard around. I saw it this morning, not far from the stream. No one is sure how it got here. So don't take any chances. Get home early.'

'So there really is a leopard,' said Sonu.

They took his advice and walked faster, and Sonu forgot to complain about his aching feet.

They were home well before sunset.

There was a smell of cooking in the air and they were hungry.

'Cabbage and roti,' said Prakash gloomily. 'But I could eat anything today.' He stopped outside his small slate-roofed house, and Bina and Sonu waved him goodbye, then carried on across a couple of ploughed fields until they reached their small stone house.

'Stuffed tomatoes,' said Sonu, sniffing just outside the front door.

'And lemon pickle,' said Bina, who had helped cut, sun and salt the lemons a month previously.

Their mother was lighting the kitchen stove. They greeted her with great hugs and demands for an immediate dinner. She was a good cook who could make even the simplest of dishes taste delicious. Her favourite saying was, 'Home-made pai is better than chicken soup in Delhi,' and Bina and Sonu had to agree.

Electricity had yet to reach their village, and they took their meal by the light of a kerosene lamp. After the meal, Sonu settled down to do a little homework, while Bina stepped outside to look at the stars.

Across the fields, someone was playing a flute. 'It must be Prakash,' thought Bina. 'He always breaks off on the high notes.' But the flute music was simple and appealing, and she began singing softly to herself in the dark.

4

Mr Mani was having trouble with the porcupines. They had been getting into his garden at night and digging up and eating his potatoes. From his bedroom window—left open, now that the mild-April weather had arrived—he could listen to them enjoying the vegetables he had worked hard to grow. Scrunch, scrunch! *Katar, katar!* Their sharp teeth sliced through the largest and juiciest of potatoes. For Mr Mani, it was as though they were biting through his own flesh. And the sound of them digging industriously as they rooted up those healthy, leafy plants, made him tremble with rage and indignation. The unfairness of it all!

Yes, Mr Mani hated porcupines. He prayed for their destruction, their removal from the face of the earth. But, as his friends were quick to point out, 'Bhagwan protected porcupines too,' and in any case you could never see the creatures or catch them, they were completely nocturnal.

Mr Mani got out of bed every night, torch in one hand, a stout stick in the other, but as soon as he stepped into the garden, the crunching and digging stopped and he was greeted by the most infuriating of silences. He would grope around in the dark, swinging wildly with the stick, but not a single porcupine was to be seen or heard. As soon as he was back in bed—the sounds would start all over again. Scrunch, scrunch, *katar, katar*...

Mr Mani came to his class tired and dishevelled, with rings beneath his eyes and a permanent frown on his face. It took some time for his pupils to discover the reason for his misery, but when they did, they felt sorry for their teacher and took to discussing ways and means of saving his potatoes from the porcupines.

It was Prakash who came up with the idea of a moat or waterditch. 'Porcupines don't like water,' he said knowledgeably.

'How do you know?' asked one of his friends.

'Throw water on one and see how it runs! They don't like getting their quills wet.'

There was no one who could disprove Prakash's theory, and the class fell in with the idea of building a moat, especially as it meant getting most of the day off.

'Anything to make Mr Mani happy,' said the headmaster, and the rest of the school watched with envy as the pupils of Class Five, armed with spades and shovels collected from all parts of the village, took up their positions around Mr Mani's potato field and began digging a ditch.

By evening the moat was ready, but it was still dry and the porcupines got in again that night and had a great feast.

'At this rate,' said Mr Mani gloomily 'there won't be any potatoes left to save.'

But next day Prakash and the other boys and girls managed to divert the water from a stream that flowed past the village. They had the satisfaction of watching it flow gently into the ditch. Everyone went home in a good mood. By nightfall, the ditch had overflowed, the potato field was flooded, and

Mr Mani found himself trapped inside his house. But Prakash and his friends had won the day. The porcupines stayed away that night!

A month had passed, and wild violets, daisies and buttercups now sprinkled the hill slopes, and on her way to school Bina gathered enough to make a little posy. The bunch of flowers fitted easily into an old ink-well. Miss Ramola was delighted to find this little display in the middle of her desk.

'Who put these here?' she asked in surprise.

Bina kept quiet, and the rest of the class smiled secretively. After that, they took turns bringing flowers for the classroom.

On her long walks to school and home again, Bina became aware that April was the month of new leaves. The oak leaves were bright green above and silver beneath, and when they rippled in the breeze they were like clouds of silvery green. The path was strewn with old leaves, dry and crackly. Sonu loved kicking them around.

Clouds of white butterflies floated across the stream. Sonu was chasing a butterfly when he stumbled over something dark and repulsive. He went sprawling on the grass. When he got to his feet, he looked down at the remains of a small animal.

'Bina! Prakash! Come quickly!' he shouted.

It was part of a sheep, killed some days earlier by a much larger animal.

'Only a leopard could have done this,' said Prakash.

'Let's get away, then,' said Sonu. 'It might still be around!'

'No, there's nothing left to eat. The leopard will be hunting elsewhere by now. Perhaps it's moved on to the next valley.'

'Still, I'm frightened,' said Sonu. 'There might be more leopards!'

Bina took him by the hand. 'Leopards don't attack humans!' she said.

'They will, if they get a taste for people!' insisted Prakash.

'Well, this one hasn't attacked any people as yet,' said Bina, although she couldn't be sure. Hadn't there been rumours of a leopard attacking some workers near the dam? But she did not want Sonu to feel afraid, so she did not mention the story. All she said was, 'It has probably come here because of all the activity near the dam.'

All the same, they hurried home. And for a few days, whenever they reached the stream, they crossed over very quickly, unwilling to linger too long at that lovely spot.

5

A few days later, a school party was on its way to Tehri to see the new dam that was being built.

Miss Ramola had arranged to take her class, and Mr Mani, not wishing to be left out, insisted on taking his class as well. That meant there were about fifty boys and girls taking part in the outing. The little bus could only take thirty. A friendly truck driver agreed to take some children if they were prepared to sit on sacks of potatoes. And Prakash persuaded the owner of the diesel-roller to turn it round and head it back to Tehri—with him and a couple of friends up on the driving seat.

Prakash's small group set off at sunrise, as they had to walk some distance in order to reach the stranded road-roller.

The bus left at 9 a.m. with Miss Ramola and her class, and Mr Mani and some of his pupils. The truck was to follow later.

It was Bina's first visit to a large town and her first bus ride.

The sharp curves along the winding, downhill road made several children feel sick. The bus driver seemed to be in a tearing hurry. He took them along at rolling, rollicking speed, which made Bina feel quite giddy. She rested her head on her arms and refused to look out of the window. Hairpin bends and cliff edges, pine forests and snow-capped peaks, all swept past her, but she felt too ill to want to look at anything. It was just as well—those sudden drops, hundreds of feet to the valley below, were quite frightening. Bina began to wish that she hadn't come—or that she had joined Prakash on the road-roller instead!

Miss Ramola and Mr Mani didn't seem to notice the lurching and groaning of the old bus. They had made this journey many times. They were busy arguing about the advantages and disadvantages of large dams—an argument that was to continue on and off for much of the day; sometimes in Hindi, sometimes in English, sometimes in the local dialect!

Meanwhile, Prakash and his friends had reached the roller. The driver hadn't turned up, but they managed to reverse it and get it going in the direction of Tehri. They were soon overtaken by both the bus and the truck but kept moving along at a steady chug. Prakash spotted Bina at the window of the bus and waved cheerfully. She responded feebly.

Bina felt better when the road levelled out near Tehri. As they crossed an old bridge over the wide river, they were startled by a loud bang which made the bus shudder. A cloud of dust rose above the town.

'They're blasting the mountain,' said Miss Ramola.

'End of a mountain,' said Mr Mani mournfully.

While they were drinking cups of tea at the bus stop, waiting for the potato truck and the road-roller, Miss Ramola and Mr Mani continued their argument about the dam. Miss Ramola maintained that it would bring electric power and water for irrigation to large areas of the country, including the surrounding area. Mr Mani declared that it was a menace, as it was situated in an earthquake zone. There would be a terrible disaster if the dam burst! Bina found it all very confusing. And what about the animals in the area, she wondered, what would happen to them?

The argument was becoming quite heated when the potato truck arrived. There was no sign of the road-roller, so it was decided that Mr Mani should wait for Prakash and his friends while Miss Ramola's group went ahead.

Some eight or nine miles before Tehri, the road-roller had broken down, and Prakash and his friends were forced to walk. They had not gone far, however, when a mule train came along—five or six mules that had been delivering sacks of grain in Nauti. A boy rode on the first mule, but the others had no loads.

'Can you give us a ride to Tehri?' called Prakash.

'Make yourselves comfortable,' said the boy.

There were no saddles, only gunny sacks strapped on to the mules with rope. They had a rough but jolly ride down to the Tehri bus stop. None of them had ever ridden mules; but they had saved at least an hour on the road.

Looking around the bus stop for the rest of the party, they could find no one from their school. And Mr Mani, who should have been waiting for them, had vanished.

6

Tania Ramola and her group had taken the steep road to the hill above Tehri. Half-an-hour's climbing brought them to a little plateau which overlooked the town, the river and the dam-site.

The earthworks for the dam were only just coming up, but a wide tunnel had been bored through the mountain to divert the river into another channel. Down below, the old town was still spread out across the valley and from a distance it looked quite charming and picturesque.

'Will the whole town be swallowed up by the waters of the dam?' asked Bina.

'Yes, all of it,' said Miss Ramola. 'The clock tower and the old palace. The long bazaar, and the temples, the schools and the jail, and hundreds of houses, for many miles up the valley. All those people will have to go—thousands of them! Of course, they'll be resettled elsewhere.'

'But the town's been here for hundreds of years,' said Bina. 'They were quite happy without the dam, weren't they?'

'I suppose they were. But the dam isn't just for them—it's for the millions who live further downstream, across the plains.'

'And it doesn't matter what happens to this place?'

'The local people will be given new homes, somewhere else.' Miss Ramola found herself on the defensive and decided to change the subject. 'Everyone must be hungry. It's time we had our lunch.'

Bina kept quiet. She didn't think the local people would want to go away. And it was a good thing, she mused, that there was only a small stream and not a big river running past her village. To be uprooted like this—a town and hundreds of villages—and put down somewhere on the hot, dusty plains—seemed to her unbearable.

'Well, I'm glad I don't live in Tehri,' she said.

She did not know it, but all the animals and most of the birds had already left the area. The leopard had been among them.

They walked through the colourful, crowded bazaar, where fruit-sellers did business beside silversmiths, and pavement vendors sold everything from umbrellas to glass bangles. Sparrows attacked sacks of grain, monkeys made off with bananas, and stray cows and dogs rummaged in refuse bins, but nobody took any notice. Music blared from radios. Buses blew their horns. Sonu bought a whistle to add to the general din, but Miss Ramola told him to put it away. Bina had kept ten rupees aside, and now she used it to buy a cotton head-scarf for her mother.

As they were about to enter a small restaurant for a meal, they were joined by Prakash and his companions; but of Mr Mani there was still no sign.

'He must have met one of his relatives,' said Prakash. 'He has relatives everywhere.'

After a simple meal of rice and lentils, they walked the length of the bazaar without seeing Mr Mani. At last, when they were about to give up the search, they saw him emerge from a by-lane, a large sack slung over his shoulder.

'Sir, where have you been?' asked Prakash. 'We have been looking for you everywhere.'

On Mr Mani's face was a look of triumph.

'Help me with this bag,' he said breathlessly.

'You've bought more potatoes, sir,' said Prakash.

'Not potatoes, boy. Dahlia bulbs!'

7

It was dark by the time they were all back in Nauti. Mr Mani had refused to be separated from his sack of dahlia bulbs, and had been forced to sit in the back of the truck with Prakash and most of the boys.

Bina did not feel so ill on the return journey. Going uphill was definitely better than going downhill! But by the time the bus reached Nauti it was too late for most of the children to walk back to the more distant villages. The boys were put up in different homes, while the girls were given beds in the school veranda.

The night was warm and still. Large moths fluttered around the single bulb that lit the veranda. Counting moths, Sonu soon fell asleep. But Bina stayed awake for some time, listening to the sounds of the night. A nightjar went *tonk-tonk* in the bushes, and somewhere in the forest an owl hooted softly. The sharp call of a barking deer travelled up the valley, from the direction of the stream. Jackals kept howling. It seemed that there were more of them than ever before.

Bina was not the only one to hear the barking deer. The leopard, stretched full length on a rocky ledge, heard it too. The leopard raised its head and then got up slowly. The deer was its natural prey. But there weren't many left, and that was why the leopard, robbed of its forest by the dam, had taken to attacking dogs and cattle near the villages.

As the cry of the barking deer sounded nearer, the leopard left its lookout point and moved swiftly through the shadows towards the stream.

8

In early June the hills were dry and dusty, and forest fires broke out, destroying shrubs and trees, killing birds and small animals. The resin in the pines made these trees burn more fiercely, and the wind would take sparks from the trees and carry them into the dry grass and leaves, so that new fires would spring up before the old ones had died out. Fortunately, Bina's village was not in the pine belt; the fires did not reach it. But Nauti was surrounded by a fire that raged for three days, and the children had to stay away from school.

And then, towards the end of June, the monsoon rains arrived and there was an end to forest fires. The monsoon lasts three months and the lower Himalayas would be drenched in rain, mist and cloud for the next three months.

The first rain arrived while Bina, Prakash and Sonu were returning home from school. Those first few drops on the dusty path made them cry out with excitement. Then the rain grew heavier and a wonderful aroma rose from the earth.

'The best smell in the world!' exclaimed Bina.

Everything suddenly came to life. The grass, the crops, the trees, the birds. Even the leaves of the trees glistened and looked new.

That first wet weekend, Bina and Sonu helped their mother plant beans, maize and cucumbers. Sometimes, when the rain was very heavy, they had to run indoors. Otherwise they worked in the rain, the soft mud clinging to their bare legs.

Prakash now owned a black dog with one ear up and one ear down. The dog ran around getting in everyone's way, barking at cows, goats, hens and humans, without frightening any of them. Prakash said it was a very clever dog, but no one else seemed to think so. Prakash also said it would protect the village from the leopard, but others said the dog would be the first to be taken—he'd run straight into the jaws of Mr Spots!

In Nauti, Tania Ramola was trying to find a dry spot in the quarters she'd been given. It was an old building and the roof was leaking in several places. Mugs and buckets were scattered about the floor in order to catch the drip.

Mr Mani had dug up all his potatoes and presented them to the friends and neighbours who had given him lunches and dinners. He was having the time of his life, planting dahlia bulbs all over his garden.

'I'll have a field of many-coloured dahlias!' he announced. 'Just wait till the end of August!'

'Watch out for those porcupines,' warned his sister. 'They eat dahlia bulbs too!'

Mr Mani made an inspection tour of his moat, no longer in flood, and found everything in good order. Prakash had done his job well.

Now, when the children crossed the stream, they found that the water-level had risen by about a foot. Small cascades had turned into waterfalls. Ferns had sprung up on the banks. Frogs chanted.

Prakash and his dog dashed across the stream. Bina and

Sonu followed more cautiously. The current was much stronger now and the water was almost up to their knees. Once they had crossed the stream, they hurried along the path, anxious not to be caught in a sudden downpour.

By the time they reached school, each of them had two or three leeches clinging to their legs. They had to use salt to remove them. The leeches were the most troublesome part of the rainy season. Even the leopard did not like them. It could not lie in the long grass without getting leeches on its paws and face.

One day, when Bina, Prakash and Sonu were about to cross the stream they heard a low rumble, which grew louder every second. Looking up at the opposite hill, they saw several trees shudder, tilt outwards and begin to fall. Earth and rocks bulged out from the mountain, then came crashing down into the ravine.

'Landslide!' shouted Sonu.

'It's carried away the path,' said Bina. 'Don't go any further.'

There was a tremendous roar as more rocks, trees and bushes fell away and crashed down the hillside.

Prakash's dog, who had gone ahead, came running back, tail between his legs.

They remained rooted to the spot until the rocks had stopped falling and the dust had settled. Birds circled the area, calling wildly. A frightened barking deer ran past them.

'We can't go to school now,' said Prakash. 'There's no way around.'

They turned and trudged home through the gathering mist.

In Koli, Prakash's parents had heard the roar of the landslide. They were setting out in search of the children when they saw them emerge from the mist, waving cheerfully.

9

They had to miss school for another three days, and Bina was afraid they might not be able to take their final exams. Although Prakash was not really troubled at the thought of missing exams, he did not like feeling helpless just because their path had been swept away. So he explored the hillside until he found a goat-track going around the mountain. It joined up with another path near Nauti. This made their walk longer by a mile, but Bina did not mind. It was much cooler now that the rains were in full swing.

The only trouble with the new route was that it passed close to the leopard's lair. The animal had made this area its own since being forced to leave the dam area.

One day Prakash's dog ran ahead of them, barking furiously. Then he ran back, whimpering.

'He's always running away from something,' observed Sonu. But a minute later he understood the reason for the dog's fear.

They rounded a bend and Sonu saw the leopard standing in their way. They were struck dumb—too terrified to run. It was a strong, sinewy creature. A low growl rose from its throat. It seemed ready to spring.

They stood perfectly still, afraid to move or say a word. And the leopard must have been equally surprised. It stared at them for a few seconds, then bounded across the path and into the oak forest.

Sonu was shaking. Bina could hear her heart hammering. Prakash could only stammer: 'Did you see the way he sprang? Wasn't he beautiful?'

He forgot to look at his watch for the rest of the day.

A few days later Sonu stopped and pointed to a large outcrop of rock on the next hill.

The leopard stood far above them, outlined against the sky. It looked strong, majestic. Standing beside it were two young cubs.

'Look at those little ones!' exclaimed Sonu.

'So it's a female, not a male,' said Prakash.

'That's why she was killing so often,' said Bina. 'She had to feed her cubs too.'

They remained still for several minutes, gazing up at the leopard and her cubs. The leopard family took no notice of them.

'She knows we are here,' said Prakash, 'but she doesn't care. She knows we won't harm them.'

'We are cubs too!' said Sonu.

'Yes,' said Bina. 'And there's still plenty of space for all of us. Even when the dam is ready there will still be room for leopards and humans.'

10

The school exams were over. The rains were nearly over too. The landslide had been cleared, and Bina, Prakash and Sonu were once again crossing the stream.

There was a chill in the air, for it was the end of September.

Prakash had learnt to play the flute quite well, and he played on the way to school and then again on the way home. As a result he did not look at his watch so often.

One morning they found a small crowd in front of Mr Mani's house.

'What could have happened?' wondered Bina. 'I hope he hasn't got lost again.'

'Maybe he's sick,' said Sonu.

'Maybe it's the porcupines,' said Prakash.

But it was none of these things.

Mr Mani's first dahlia was in bloom, and half the village had turned out to look at it! It was a huge red double dahlia, so heavy that it had to be supported with sticks. No one had ever seen such a magnificent flower!

Mr Mani was a happy man. And his mood only improved over the coming week, as more and more dahlias flowered—crimson, yellow, purple, mauve, white—button dahlias, pompom dahlias, spotted dahlias, striped dahlias... Mr Mani had them all! A dahlia even turned up on Tania Romola's desk—he got on quite well with her now—and another brightened up the headmaster's study.

A week later, on their way home—it was almost the last day of the school term—Bina, Prakash and Sonu talked about what they might do when they grew up.

'I think I'll become a teacher,' said Bina. 'I'll teach children about animals and birds, and trees and flowers.'

'Better than maths!' said Prakash.

'I'll be a pilot,' said Sonu. 'I want to fly a plane like Miss Ramola's brother.'

'And what about you, Prakash?' asked Bina.

Prakash just smiled and said, 'Maybe I'll be a flute-player,' and he put the flute to he lips and played a sweet melody.

'Well, the world needs flute-players too,' said Bina, as they fell into step beside him.

The leopard had been stalking a barking deer. She paused when she heard the flute and the voices of the children. Her own young ones were growing quickly, but the girl and the two boys did not look much older.

They had started singing their favourite song again.

Five more miles to go!
We climb through rain and snow,
A river to cross...
A mountain to pass...
Now we've four more miles to go!

The leopard waited until they had passed, before returning to the trail of the barking deer.

A tree says:
A kernel is
hidden in me,
a spark,
a thought,
I am life
from
eternal life

The Coconut Tree

The beginnings of most cultivated plants are a mystery, and few have received as much attention from scientists and botanists as the familiar coconut palm.

Though it cannot be proved that the coconut first originated in India, there is no doubt that this tree has been with us since earliest times. Mention is made of it in several of the Puranas, which are the oldest books after the Vedas. There is also mention of it in the Ramayana and the Mahabharata as well as in ancient Tamil literature. In some Hindu ceremonies, worship is offered to Varuna, the god presiding over the water and the oceans. This god is represented by a pot of water with a coconut placed at the mouth. The offering of an unbroken coconut to the sea probably comes from the idea that the coconut came from the seas. And there is a Ceylonese legend that says that it was brought to India from Nagaloka, a blissful region beyond the seas.

The Papuans of New Guinea take pride in calling themselves the Coconut People. They hate the non-Papuans of their island who, they say, are not true Coconuts. They have a fantastic legend regarding the origin of the coconut. Even before the creation of man, their god killed another god, Somoali by name, who later became the god of the bushmen and the nomads. He placed the head of his victim on the bank of the Wamagao River, and after six nights, when he returned to see the head of his enemy, he found leaves sprouting from it. He then planted the sprouting head in the earth and from it grew the first coconut.

Most botanists seem to think that the original home of the coconut is not far from India, probably 'somewhere in the lands now under the sea, which existed in the western parts of the Indian Ocean'. All are agreed that its home is somewhere between Zanzibar and New Guinea. The seafaring Polynesians and wandering Malays probably carried it eastwards and westwards. It was probably the adventurous Polynesian mariners who first planted it in the New World.

The Malay seafarers, the once-maritime Tamils and the ancient mariners of the Bengal coast have probably been responsible for a much wider distribution of the coconut into the lands of the Indian Ocean. Ocean currents and monsoon drifts have also played a part in its spread.

So old is the plant in India that from early times the Arabs have called it the Indian Nut. Marco Polo called it by the same name. For Hindus it is the Kalpaka Vriksha, or Tree of Heaven.

Apart from the refreshing qualities of the flesh and water of the coconut fruit, this tree has many uses. In Goa, brooms are made from the leaf ribs, while in Kerala the fermented sap is known as palm wine or toddy. The sugar from the sap gives us jaggery, the fibre from the outer rind provides coir fibre, the dry fleshy kernel provides copra and the oil extracted from the dry copra gives us coconut oil or coconut butter.

Several other palms are well-known in India—the tall, slim betel-nut palm; the shaggy wild date palm; and the palmyra palm, on whose strong leaves the ancient scriptures were written.

The Friendly Oaks

When I remember the oak trees below the old cottage in the hills, I see again the long-tailed blue magpies fluttering from tree to tree; a woodpecker tapping away at the bark; brightly coloured minivets standing out against its dark foliage; and a band of langurs crashing through the branches in search of acorns. The oaks were always hospitable to birds, beasts and insects.

This is the Banj oak, growing from 5,000 ft. to 7,000 ft. in the western Himalayas. Higher up, other species of oak take over, dominating the most northern slopes facing the snows.

Oaks like each other's company, but each one has a certain individuality—its branches growing as they please, avoiding symmetry, taking on shapes that often give the tree an untidy look, as though it could do with a little discipline. But that of course, is its charm.

Our Himalayan oaks are a little different from the famous oaks of England and Europe. The mighty oak is England's noblest tree. The Romans made the crown of oak leaves (which symbolizes bravery) their principal award, and it could only be given to a citizen who had slain an enemy, won a battle or saved the life of a fellow citizen. The Celts worshipped the oak, regarding it as the symbol of their most prized virtue, hospitality.

Even the moss grows more readily on the trunks of an old oak tree.

The Cottage Called Maplewood

It isn't many years since I left Maplewood, but I wouldn't be surprised to hear that the cottage has disappeared. Already, during my last months there, the trees were being cut and a new road was being blasted out of the mountain. It would pass just below the old cottage. There were (as far as I know) no plans to blow up the house; but it was already shaky and full of cracks, and a few tremors, such as those produced by passing trucks, drilling machines and bulldozers, would soon bring the cottage to the ground.

If it has gone, don't write and tell me: I'd rather not know.

When I moved in, it had been nestling there among the oaks for over seventy years. It had become a part of the forest. Birds nestled in the eaves; beetles burrowed in the woodwork. Some denizens remained, even during my residence. And I was there—how long? Eight, nine years, I'm not sure; it was a timeless sort of place. Even the rent was paid only once a year, at a time of my choosing.

I first saw the cottage in late spring, when the surrounding forest was at its best—the oaks and maples in new leaf, the oak leaves a pale green, the maple leaves red and gold and bronze; this is the Himalayan maple, quite different from the North American maple; only the winged seed-pods are similar, twisting and turning in the breeze as they fall to the ground. The Garhwalis call it the Butterfly Tree.

There was one very tall, very old maple above the cottage, and this was probably the tree that gave the house its name. A portion of it was blackened where it had been struck by lightning, but the rest of it lived on; a favourite haunt of woodpeckers. The ancient peeling bark seemed to harbour any number of tiny insects, and the woodpeckers would be tapping away all day. A steep path ran down to the cottage. During heavy rain, it would become a watercourse and the earth would be washed away to leave it very stony and uneven. I first took this path to see Miss Mackenzie, an impoverished old lady who lived in two small rooms on the ground floor and who was acting on behalf of the owner. It was she who told me that the cottage was to-let, provided she could remain in the portion downstairs.

Actually, the path ran straight across a landing and up to the front door of the first floor. It was the ground floor that was tucked away in the shadow of the hill; it was reached by a flight of steps, which also took the rush of water when the path was in flood.

Miss Mackenzie was eighty-six. I helped her up the steps and she opened the door for me. It led into an L-shaped room. There were two large windows, and when I pushed the first of these open, the forest seemed to rush upon me. Below, from the ravine, the deep-throated song of the whistling thrush burst upon me.

I told Miss Mackenzie I would take the place. She grew excited; it must have been lonely for her during the past several years, with most of the cottage lying empty, and only her old bearer and a mongrel dog for company. Her own house had been mortgaged to a moneylender. Her brothers and sisters were long dead.

I told her I would move in soon: my books were still in Delhi. She gave me the keys and I left a cheque with her. It was all done on an impulse—the decision to give up my job in Delhi, find a cheap house in a hill-station, and return to freelance writing. It was a dream I'd had for some time; lack of money had made it difficult to realize. But then, I knew that if I was going to wait for money to come, I might have to wait until I was old and grey and full of sleep. I was thirty-five—still young enough to take a few risks. If the dream was to become reality, this was the time to do something about it.

I don't know what led me to Maplewood; it was the first place I saw, and I did not bother to see any others. The location was far from being ideal. It faced east, and stood in the shadow of the Balahissar Hill; so that while it received the early morning sun, it went without the evening sun.

There was no view of the snows and no view of the plains. In front stood Burnt Hill. But the forest below the cottage seemed full of possibilities, and the windows opening on to it probably decided the issue. In my romantic frame of mind, I was susceptible to magic casements opening wide. I would make a window-seat and lie there on a summer's day, writing lyric poetry...

But long before that could happen I was opening tins of sardines and sharing them with Miss Mackenzie. And then Prem came along. And there were others, like Binya. I went away at times, but returned as soon as possible. Once you have lived with mountains, there is no escape. You belong to them.

When the Chestnuts Fall

When the horse-chestnut comes into new leaf, we know that spring has come to the hills. And by the end of April these handsome trees are festooned with candelabra of lovely pink blossom. Then, during the rains, the chestnuts begin to form. By October they have split their green jackets, and shiny brown chestnuts are falling to the grounds.

Why 'horse-chestnuts'? Well, these beautiful chestnuts are not really edible, except perhaps for horses. Even the monkeys disdain them. Being destructive by nature, the rhesus monkeys will bite into the chestnut and then spit them out; they will destroy as many as they possibly can, just because they are not to their taste!

As schoolboys we collected whole chestnuts and used them to play a game called 'conkers'. You attached your chestnut to a length of string and used it to strike your opponents' chestnut in an effort to shatter it. I remember having a very strong, sturdy chestnut, which resisted all the blows it received. Such simple games are no more. Technology has robbed children of their innocence.

But I still collect chestnuts when I can find them. Plant a chestnut whole, and in the coming spring you will have the pleasure of seeing a young tree sprung up.

My Trees in the Himalayas

Living in a cottage at 7,000 ft. in the Garhwal Himalayas, I am fortunate to have a big window that opens out on the forest so that the trees are almost within my reach. If I jumped, I could land quite neatly in the arms of an oak or horse chestnut. I have never made that leap, but the big langurs—silver-grey monkeys with long, swishing tails—often spring from the trees onto my corrugated tin roof, making enough noise to frighten all the birds away.

Standing on its own outside my window is a walnut tree, and truly this is a tree for all seasons. In winter, the branches were bare; but they were smooth, straight and round like the arms of an apsara. In spring each limb produces a bright green spear of new growth, and by midsummer the entire tree is in leaf. Toward the end of the monsoon, the walnuts, encased in their green jackets, have reached maturity. When the jackets begin to split, you can see the hard brown shells of the nuts, and inside each shell is the delicious meat itself. Look closely at the nut, and you will notice that it is shaped rather like the human brain. No wonder the ancients prescribed walnuts for headaches.

Every year this tree gives me a basket of walnuts. But last

year, the nuts were disappearing one by one, and I was at a loss as to who had been taking them. Could it have been Bijju, the milkman's small son? He was an inveterate tree climber, but he was usually to be found on the oak trees, gathering fodder for his herd. He admitted that his cows had enjoyed my dahlias, which they had eaten the previous week, but he stoutly denied having fed them walnuts, saying they did not care for them.

Later, I found a fat langur sitting in the walnut tree. I watched him for some time to see if he was going to help himself to the nuts, but he was only sunning himself. When he thought I wasn't looking, he came down and ate the geraniums; but he did not take any walnuts.

It wasn't the woodpecker either. He was out there every day, knocking furiously against the bark of the tree, trying to pry an insect out of a narrow crack. He was strictly non-vegetarian and none the worse for it.

The nuts seemed to disappear early in the morning while I was still in bed, so one day I surprised everyone, including myself by getting up before sunrise. I was just in time to catch the culprit climbing out of the walnut tree. She was an old woman who sometimes came to cut grass on the hillside. Her face was as wrinkled as the walnuts she had been pinching. But in spite of her age, her arms and legs were sturdy. When she saw me, she was as swift as a civet cat in getting out of the tree.

'And how many walnuts did you gather today, Grandmother?' I asked.

'Just two,' she said with a giggle, offering them to me on her open palm. I accepted one, and thus encouraged, she climbed higher into the tree and helped herself to the remaining nuts. It was impossible for me to object. I was taken with admiration for her agility. She must have been twice my age, but I knew I could never get up that tree. To the victor, the spoils!

Last winter the PWD decided to take a new road past my doorstep, and the first casualty was the walnut tree. Along with a large number of different trees growing below the cottage, it fell to the contractors' axes.

Recently when I met the old woman on the road, I asked her, 'Where do you get your walnuts now, Grandmother?'

'Nowhere,' she answered stoically. 'That was the last walnut tree on the hillside.'

Unlike the prized walnuts, the horse chestnuts are inedible. Even the rhesus monkeys throw them away in disgust. But the tree itself is a friendly one, especially in summer when it is in full leaf. The lightest breeze makes the leaves break into conversation, and their rustle is a cheerful sound. The spring flowers of the horse chestnut look like candelabra, and when the blossoms fall, they carpet the hillside with their pale pink petals. It stands erect and dignified and does not bend with the wind. In spring, the new leaves, or needles, are a tender green, while during the monsoon, the tiny young cones spread like blossoms in the dark green folds of the branches.

The deodar enjoys the company of its own kind: where one deodar grows, there will be others. A walk in a deodar forest is awe-inspiring—surrounded on all sides by these great sentinels of the mountains, you feel as though the trees themselves are on the march.

I walk among the trees outside my window often,

acknowledging their presence with a touch of my hand against their trunks. The oak has been there the longest, and the wind has bent its upper branches and twisted a few so that it looks shaggy and undistinguished. But it is a good tree for the privacy of birds. Sometimes it seems completely uninhabited until there is a whining sound, as of a helicopter approaching, and a party of long-tailed blue magpies flies across the forest glade.

Most of the pines near my home are on the next hillside. But there is a small Himalayan blue a little way below the cottage, and sometimes I sit beneath it to listen to the wind playing softly in its branches.

When I open the window at night, there is almost always something to listen to—the mellow whistle of a pygmy owlet, or the sharp cry of a barking deer. Sometimes, if I am lucky, I will see the moon coming up over the next mountain, and two distant deodars in perfect silhouette.

Some night sounds outside my window remain strange and mysterious. Perhaps they are the sounds of the trees themselves, stretching their limbs in the dark, shifting a little, flexing their fingers, whispering to one another. These great trees of the mountains, I feel they know me well, as I watch them and listen to their secrets, happy to rest my head beneath their outstretched arms.

The Rhododendrons

We cannot leave the hills without first having a glimpse of the rhododendrons in flower. But for this you will have to visit a hill-station towards the end of March, when it is still winter in the Himalayan foothills.

When, as a boy, I went to a boarding school in Shimla, the little narrow-gauge train would come huffing and puffing up the steep incline towards Summerhill, and we would look out of the windows to admire the scarlet blossoms of the rhododendrons. For eight years of boarding school life we would be brought up the mountains by a little steam-engine, and always the rhododendrons were there to welcome us. Sometimes there was snow on the ground, and the fallen petals would stand out against the snow—scarlet against white.

Dalhousie is especially blessed with rhododendrons; at least it was, when I was last there, fifty years ago! So are the northern slopes of Mussoorie. The hill people call the flower 'baras'; it makes a good wine, if the juice is fermented by a good winemaker.

When Gautam was small, he was having some difficulty with the word 'rhododendron', so to amuse him, I played on the word:

'One rode a horse,' I said, 'and the other rhododendron!'

'Can you ride on a rhododendron?' he asked, not to be fooled.

'Maybe not', I said, 'but you can make jam with it.'

That aroused his interest, and we got his mother to make us rhododendron jam. It went down quite well; but you'll have to ask his mother for the recipe.

As you go further up in the Himalayas, you will find other varieties of the rhododendron—smaller trees with flowers coming in white, yellow, purple, and other shades. These sturdy trees, sometimes forming small forests, can be found up to 8,000 ft. in Himachal, Kumaon, Garhwal, and Kashmir. Others are found at elevations of 10,000 to 14,000 ft. in the Sutlej valley, while the rare white Rhododendron Falconeri makes its home at a similar altitude in Kashmir.

Now grown as an ornamental tree or shrub in Europe, the rhododendrons are truly at home in the Himalayas.

But why such a long name, Gautam wants to know.

Well it came from the Greek (via Latin) into English: *rhodon* meaning rose + *dendron*, meaning tree. So let's simply call it the Rose Tree!

Rhododendrons in the Mist

Blood-red, the fallen blossoms lay on the snow, even more striking when laid bare. On the trees they blended with the foliage. On the ground, on those patches of recent snow, they seemed to be bleeding.

It had been a harsh winter in the hills, and it was still snowing at the end of March. But this was flowering time for the rhododendron trees, and they blossomed in sun, snow, or pelting rain. By mid-afternoon the hill station was shrouded in a heavy mist, and the trees stood out like ghostly sentinels.

The hill station wasn't Simla, where I had gone to school, or Mussoorie, where I was to settle later on. It was Dalhousie, a neglected and almost forgotten hill station in the western Himalaya. But Dalhousie had the best rhododendron trees, and they grew all over the mountain, showing off before the colourless oaks and drooping pines.

But I wasn't in Dalhousie for the rhododendrons. It was 1959, and the Dalai Lama had just fled from Tibet, seeking sanctuary in India. Thousands of his followers and fellow-Tibetans had fled with him, and these refugees had to be settled somewhere. Dalhousie, with its many empty houses, was ideal for this purpose, and a carpet-weaving centre had been set up on one of the estates. The Tibetans made beautiful rugs and carpets. I know nothing about carpet-weaving, but I was working for CARE, an American relief organization, and I had been sent to Dalhousie (with the approval of the Government of India) to assess the needs of the refugees.

This is not the story of my tryst with the Tibetans, although I did suffer greatly from drinking large quantities of butter tea, which travels very slowly down the gullet and feels like lead by the time it reaches your stomach. The carpet-weaving centre became a great success, and I went on to work for CARE for several years; but that's another story. Out of one experience came another experience, as often happens during our peregrinations on planet Earth, and it was during my stay in Dalhousie that I had a strange and rather unsettling experience.

I was staying at a small hotel that was quite empty as no one visited Dalhousie in those days and certainly not at the end of March. The hill station had been convenient for visitors from Lahore, but Partition had put an end to that.

◆

The hotel had a small garden, bare at this time of the year. But on the second day of my stay, returning from the carpet-weaving centre, I noticed that there was a gardener working on the flower beds, digging around and transplanting some seedlings. He looked up as I passed, and for a moment I thought I knew him. There was something familiar about his features—the slit eyes, the broad, flattened nose, the harelip—yes, the cleft lip was very noticeable—but he wasn't anyone I knew or had known. At least I didn't think so…. He was just a likeness to someone

I had seen somehow, somewhere else. It was a bit of a tease.

And it would have remained just that if he hadn't looked up and met my gaze.

A flood of recognition crossed his face. But then he looked away, almost as though he did not want to recognize me; or be recognized.

I passed him. It was curious, but it didn't bother me. We keep bumping into people who look slightly familiar. It is said that everyone has a double somewhere on this planet. I had yet to meet mine—God forbid!—but perhaps I was seeing someone else's double.

I was relaxing in the veranda later that evening, browsing through an old magazine, when the gardener passed me on his way to the garden shed to put away his tools. There was something about his walk that brought back an image from the past. He had a slight limp. And when he looked at me again, his harelip registered itself on my memory. And now I recognized him. And of course he knew me.

I was the man who'd caught him rifling through my landlady's cupboards and drawers in Dehradun, some three years previously. I had exposed him, reported him, suggested she dismiss him; but the old lady, a widow, had grown quite fond of the youth, and had kept him in her service. He was good at running about and making himself useful, and, in spite of his cleft lip, he was not unattractive.

When I left Dehradun to take up my job in Delhi, I had forgotten the matter, almost forgotten the young man and my landlady; it was another tenant who informed me that the youth—his name was Sohan—had stabbed the old lady and made off with the contents of her jewel case and other valuables. She had died in hospital a few days later.

Sohan hadn't been caught. He had obviously left the town and taken to the hills or a large city. The police had made sporadic attempts to locate him, but as time passed the case lost its urgency. The victim was not a person of importance. The criminal was a stranger, a shadowy figure of no known background.

But here he was three years later, staring me in the face. What was I to do about him? Or what was he to do about me?

◆

After Sohan had gone to his quarters, somewhere behind the hotel, I went in search of the manager. I would tell him what I knew and together we could decide on a course of action. But he had gone to a marriage and would be back late. The hotel was in charge of the cook who, a little drunk, served dinner in a hurry and retired to his quarters. 'Don't you have a night-watchman?' I asked him before he took off. 'Yes, of course,' he replied, 'Sohan, the gardener. He's the chowkidar too!'

An early retirement seemed the best thing all round, especially as I had to leave the next day. So I went to my room and made sure all the doors and windows were locked. I pushed the inside bolts all the way. I made sure the antiquated window frames were locked. As I peered out of the window, I noticed that a heavy mist had descended on the hillside. The trees stood out like ghostly apparitions, here and there a rhododendron glowing like the embers of a small fire. Then darkness enveloped the hillside. I felt cold, and wondered how much of it was fear.

I went to the bathroom and bolted the back door. Now no one could get in. Even so, I felt uneasy. Sohan was still a fugitive from the law, I had recognized him, and I was a threat to his freedom. He had killed once—perhaps more than once—and he could kill again.

I read for some time, then put out the light and tried to sleep. From a distance came the strains of music from a wedding band. Someone knocked on the door. I switched on the light and looked at my watch. It was only 10 p.m. Perhaps the manager had returned.

There was another knock, and I went to the door and was about to open it when some childhood words of warning from my grandmother came to mind: 'Never open the door unless you know who's there!'

'Who's there?' I called.

No answer. Just another knock.

'Who's there?' I called again.

There was a cough, a double-rap on the door.

'I'm sleeping,' I said. 'Come in the morning.' And I returned to my bed. The knocking continued but I ignored it, and after some time the person went away.

I slept a little. A couple of hours must have passed when I was woken by further knocking. But it did not come from the door. It was above me, high up on the wall. I'd forgotten there was a skylight.

I switched on the light and looked up. A face was outlined against the glass of the skylight. I could make out the flat rounded face and the harelip. It appeared to be grinning at me—rather like the disembodied head of the Cheshire cat in *Alice in Wonderland*.

The skylight was very small and I knew he couldn't crawl through the opening. But he could show me a knife—and that was what he did. It was a small clasp knife and he held it between his teeth as he peered down at me. I felt very vulnerable on the bed. So I switched off the light and moved to an old sofa at the far end of the room, where I couldn't be seen. There didn't seem to be any point in shouting for help. So I just sat there, waiting…. And presumably, without a sound, he slipped away, and I remained on the sofa until the first glimmer of dawn penetrated the drawn window curtains.

♦

The manager was apologetic. 'You should have rung the bell,' he said, 'someone would have come.'

'The bell doesn't work. And someone did come…'

'I'm sorry, I'm sorry. The fellow's a villain, no doubt about it. And he's missing this morning. Your presence here must have frightened him off. So he's wanted for theft and murder. Well, we shall inform the police. Perhaps they can pick him up before he leaves the town.'

And we did inform the police. But Sohan had already taken off. The milkman had seen him boarding the early morning bus to Pathankot.

Pathankot was a busy little town on the plain below Dehradun. From there one road goes to Jammu, another to Dharamsala, a narrow-gauge railway to Kangra, and the main railway to Amritsar or Delhi. Sohan could have taken any of those routes. And no one was going to go looking for him. A police alert would be put out—a mere formality. He wasn't on their list of current criminals.

That afternoon I took a taxi to Pathankot and whiled away the evening at the railway station. My train, an overnight express to Delhi, left at 8 p.m. There was no rush at that time of the year. I had a first-class compartment to myself.

In those days our trains were somewhat different from what they are today. A first, second or third class compartment was usually a single carriage, or bogey. We did not have corridor trains. Bogeys were connected by steel couplings, otherwise you were not connected in any way to the other compartments. But there was an emergency cord above the upper berths, and if you pulled it, the train might stop. There were always troublemakers on the trains, just as there are today, and sometimes the chain was pulled out of mischief. As a result it was often ignored.

As the train began moving out of the station I went to all the windows and made sure that they were fastened. Then I bolted the carriage door. I was becoming adept at bolting doors and windows. Sohan was probably hiding out in some distant town or village, but I wasn't taking any chances.

The train gathered speed. The lights of Pathankot receded as we plunged into a dark and moonless night. I had a pillow and a blanket with me, and I stretched out on one of the bunks and tried to think about pleasant things such as scarlet geraniums, fragrant sweet peas, and the beautiful Nimmi, star of the silver screen; but instead I kept seeing the grinning face of a young man with a harelip. All the same, I drifted into sleep. The rocking movement of the carriage, the rhythm of the wheels on the rails, have always had a soothing effect on my nerves. I sleep well in trains and rocking chairs.

But not that night.

I woke to the sound of that familiar tapping; not at the door, but on the window glass not far from my head. The insistent tapping of someone who wanted to get in.

It was common enough for ticketless travellers to hang on to the carriage of a moving train, in the hope that someone would let them in. But they usually chose the crowded second or third-class compartments; a first-class traveller, often alone, was unlikely to let in a stranger who might well turn out to be a train robber.

I raised my head from my pillow, and there he was, clinging to the fast-moving train, his face pressed to the glass, his harelip revealing part of a broken tooth.... I pulled down the shutters, blotting out his face. But, agile as a cat, he moved to the next window, the sneer still on his face. I pulled down that shutter too.

I pulled down all the shutters on his side of the carriage. He couldn't get in, bodily. But mentally, he was all over me.

Mind over matter. Well, I could apply my mind too. I shut my eyes and willed my tormentor to fall off the train!

No one fell off the train (at least no one was reported to have done so), but presently we slowed to a gradual stop and, when I pulled up the shutters of the window, I saw that we were at a station. Jalandhar, I think. The platform was brightly lit and there was no sign of Sohan. He must have jumped off the train as it slowed down. It was about one in the morning.

A vendor brought me a welcome glass of hot tea, and life returned to normal.

◆

I did not see Sohan in the years that followed. Or rather, I saw many Sohans. For two or three years I was pursued by my 'familiar'. Wherever I went—and my work took me to different parts of the country—I found myself encountering young men with harelips and a menacing look. Pure imagination, of course. He had every reason to stay as far from me as possible.

Gradually, the 'sightings' died down. Young men with harelips became extremely rare. Perhaps they were all going in for corrective surgery.

The years passed, and I had forgotten my familiar. I had given up my job in Delhi and moved to the hills. I was a moderately successful writer, and a familiar figure on Mussoorie's Mall Road. Sometimes other writers came to see me, in my cottage under the deodars. One of them invited me to have dinner with him at the old Regal hotel, where he was staying. Before dinner, he took me to the bar for a drink.

'What will you have, whisky or vodka?'

No one seemed to drink anything else. I asked for some dark rum, and the barman went off in search of a bottle. When he returned and began pouring my drink, I noticed something slightly familiar about his features, his stance. He was almost bald, and he had a grey, drooping moustache that concealed most of his upper lip. He glanced at me and our eyes met. There was no sign of recognition. He smiled politely as he poured my drink. No, it definitely wasn't Sohan. He was too refined, for one thing. And he went about his duties without another glance in my direction.

Dinner over, I thanked my writer friend for his hospitality, and took the long walk home to my cottage. It was a dark, moonless night. No one followed me, no one came tapping on my bedroom window.

◆

Mussoorie had its charms. In my mind, every hill station is symbolized by a particular tree, even if it's not the dominant one. Dalhousie has its rhododendrons, Simla its deodars, Kasauli its pines, and Mussoorie its horse chestnuts. The monkeys would do their best to destroy the chestnuts, but I would collect those that were whole and plant them in people's gardens, whether they wanted them or not. The horse chestnut is a lovely tree to look at, even if you can't do anything with it!

My walks took me to the Regal from time to time, and occasionally I would relax in the bar, chatting to an old resident or a casual visitor, while the barman poured me a rum and soda. He never looked twice at me. And I never saw him outside that barroom. He appeared to be as much of a fixture as the moth-eaten antler-head on the wall, only he wasn't quite as moth-eaten.

'Efficient chap,' said Colonel Bhushan indicating the barman. 'And a great favourite with his mistress.'

'You mean the owner of this place?' I had only a vague idea of who owned what in the town. And in some cases the ownership was rather vague. But in the case of the Regal— Mrs Kapoor, a wealthy widow in her fifties, was very much in charge, all too visible an owner; well fleshed-out, ample-bosomed, with arms like rolling pins. Her staff trembled at her approach; but not, it seemed, the bartender, who led a charmed life, incapable of doing any wrong.

The lights went out, as they frequently do in this technological age, and the barman brought over our next round of drinks by candlelight.

By the light of a candle I caught a glimpse of the barman's features as he hovered over me. There was only the hint of a harelip, and the candle lit up his slanting eyes and prominent cheekbones. This was the only time I had a really close look at him.

◆

A week later I met Colonel Bhushan on the Mall. This was where all the gossip took place.

'Have you heard what happened last night at the Regal?' He wasted no time in getting to the news of the day.

A twinge of fear, of anticipation, ran through me. 'Nothing too terrible, I hope?'

'That barman chap—always thought he was a bit too smooth—stabbed the old lady, stabbed her two or three times, then plundered her room and made off with jewellery worth lakhs—as well as all the cash he could find!'

'How's the lady?'

'She'll survive. Tough old buffalo. But the rascal got away. By now he must be in Sirmur, or even across the Nepal border. Probably belongs to some criminal tribe.'

Yes, I thought, possibly a descendant of one of those robber gangs who harassed pilgrims on their way to the sacred shrines, or plundered traders from Tibet, or caravans to Samarkand...To rob and plunder still runs in the blood of the most harmless-looking people.

So the barman at the Regal was the same man I'd known in Dehradun and then encountered in Dalhousie. The passing of time had altered his features but not his way of life. By now he would probably be far from Mussoorie. But I had a feeling I'd see him again—if not here, then somewhere else. Each one of us had a 'familiar'—a presence we would rather do without—an unwelcome and menacing guest—and for me it is Sohan.

Where does he come from, where does he go? I doubt if I shall ever know.

But I have a feeling he'll turn up again one of these days. And then?

Trees are
poems that
the earth
writes upon
the sky

The Indian Coral Tree

One of my earliest stories, written over sixty years ago, was about talking to a small girl who was sitting on a coral tree, showering petals on my head, and telling me what she was going to do with her life. I did not see her again, but she seemed a very determined little girl and I'm sure she did something unusual like becoming a writer or an ambassador or a ballet dancer. If you can climb trees, you'll get somewhere in life.

Coral trees are so pretty. They grow fast but they're not too big. They grow in the wild, and they will also grow in your garden or on the roadside. I wish there were more of them. Their lovely spikes of coral-red blossoms will brighten up a hillside or a field or a backyard. The flowers have no scent, but their nectar attracts all kinds of birds—crows, mynas, parakeets, babblers, bulbuls...And watch out for the bees! There's never a dull moment when the coral tree is in bloom.

Last month, on my way by road from the Jolly Grant airport to Dehradun, I caught a glimpse of a coral tree in bloom, and I remembered the girl in the tree, long, long ago. I suppose she's an old lady now. I wonder if she still climbs trees...

Going Everywhere

The night had been hot, the rain frequent, and I slept on the veranda instead of in the house. I was in my twenties and I had begun to earn a living and felt I had certain responsibilities. In a short while, a tonga would take me to a railway station, and from there a train would take me to Bombay, and then a ship would take me to England. There would be work, interviews, a job, a different kind of life; so many things that this small bungalow of my grandfather's would be remembered fitfully, in rare moments of reflection.

When I awoke on the veranda, I saw a grey morning, smelt the rain on the red earth, and remembered that I had to go away. A girl was standing on the veranda porch, looking at me very seriously. When I saw her, I sat up in bed with a start.

She was a small, dark girl, her eyes big and black, her pigtails tied up with a bright red ribbon; and she was fresh and clean like the rain and the red earth.

She stood looking at me, and she was very serious.

'Hello,' I said, smiling, trying to put her at ease.

But the girl was businesslike. She acknowledged my greeting with a brief nod.

'Can I do anything for you?' I asked, stretching my limbs. 'Do you stay near here?'

She nodded again.

'With your parents?'

With great assurance she said, 'Yes. But I can stay on my own.'

'You're like me,' I said, and for a while I forgot about being an old man of twenty. 'I like to do things on my own. I'm going away today.'

'Oh,' she said, a little breathlessly.

'Would you care to go to England?'

'I want to go everywhere,' she said, 'to America and Africa and Japan and Honolulu.'

'Maybe you will,' I said. 'I'm going everywhere, and no one can stop me... But what is it you want? What did you come for?'

'I want some flowers but I can't reach them.' She waved her hand towards the garden. 'That tree, see?'

The coral tree stood in front of the house surrounded by pools of water and broken, fallen blossoms. The branches of the tree were thick with the scarlet, pea-shaped flowers.

'All right,' I said. 'Just let me get ready.'

The tree was easy to climb, and I made myself comfortable on one of the lower branches, smiling down at the serious upturned face of the girl.

'I'll throw them down to you,' I said.

I bent a branch but the wood was young and green, and I had to twist it several times before it snapped.

'I'm not sure that I ought to do this,' I said, as I dropped the flowering branch to the girl.

'Don't worry,' she said.

'Well, if you're ready to speak up for me—'

'Don't worry.'

I felt a sudden nostalgic longing for childhood and an urge to remain behind in my grandfather's house with its tangled memories and ghosts of yesteryear. But I was the only one left, and what could I do except climb coral and jackfruit trees?

'Have you many friends?' I asked.

'Oh, yes.'

'Who is the best?'

'The cook. He lets me stay in the kitchen, which is more interesting than the house. And I like to watch him cooking. And he gives me things to eat, and tells me stories...'

'And who is your second best friend?'

She inclined her head to one side, and thought very hard.

'I'll make you the second best,' she said.

I sprinkled coral blossoms over her head. 'That's very kind of you. I'm happy to be your second best.'

A tonga bell sounded at the gate, and I looked out from the tree and said, 'It's come for me. I have to go now.'

I climbed down.

'Will you help me with my suitcases?' I asked, as we walked together towards the veranda. 'There is no one here to help me. I am the last to go. Not because I want to go, but because I have to.'

I sat down on the cot and packed a few last things in a suitcase. All the doors of the house were locked. On my way to the station I would leave the keys with the caretaker. I had already given instructions to an agent to try and sell the house. There was nothing more to be done.

We walked in silence to the waiting tonga, thinking and wondering about each other.

'Take me to the station,' I said to the tonga driver.

The girl stood at the side of the path, on the damp red earth, gazing at me.

'Thank you,' I said. 'I hope I shall see you again.'

'I'll see you in London,' she said, 'or America or Japan. I want to go everywhere.'

'I'm sure you will,' I said. 'And perhaps I'll come back and we'll meet again in this garden. That would be nice, wouldn't it?'

She nodded and smiled. We knew it was an important moment.

The tonga driver spoke to his pony, and the carriage set off down the gravel path, rattling a little. The girl and I waved to each other.

In the girl's hand was a sprig of coral blossom. As she waved, the blossoms fell apart and danced lightly in the breeze.

'Goodbye!' I called.

'Goodbye!' called the girl.

The ribbon had come loose from her pigtail and lay on the ground with the coral blossoms.

'I'm going everywhere,' I said to myself, 'and no one can stop me'.

And she was fresh and clean like the rain and the red earth.

The Jackfruit Tree

The jackfruit tree growing outside my grandmother's kitchen was very much a part of my childhood in Dehradun. But no one could tell me why it was called a 'jackfruit'. I knew all about Jack who climbed a beanstalk, but there was no story about him climbing a jackfruit tree, which would not have been very difficult. So this morning I looked up the botanical name for this handsome tree, and discovered that it was called *Artocarpus heterophyllus* by the scientists. Let's stick to jackfruit!

It really is a wonderful tree, providing both leafy shade and fruity sustenance. The fruit is large and globular; when cut open, it emits a sweet odour. Many people enjoy the ripe fruit. I have always preferred it cooked as a vegetable, the seeds and the flesh both being good to eat. And it makes a wonderful pickle! As a pickle addict, I am always on the lookout for a good jackfruit pickle.

That jackfruit tree in my grandmother's garden was a friend to me during those childhood days. I could sit on a branch and read, or just watch the squirrels come and go. And when it was time for lunch, or 'tiffin' as we called it then, I would slither down the tree trunk and tumble into the kitchen, ready to appease my schoolboy appetite.

Growing Up with Trees

Dehradun was a place for trees, and Grandfather's house was surrounded by several kinds—peepul, neem, mango, jackfruit and papaya. There was also an ancient banyan tree. I grew up amongst these trees, and some of them, planted by Grandfather, grew with me.

There were two types of trees that were of special interest to a boy—trees that were good for climbing, and trees that provided fruit.

The jackfruit tree was both these things. The fruit itself— the largest in the world—grew only on the trunk and main branches. I did not care much for the fruit, although cooked as a vegetable, it made a good curry. But the tree was large and leafy and easy to climb. It was a very dark tree and if I hid in it, I could not easily be seen from below. In a hole in the tree trunk I kept various banned items—a catapult, some lurid comics, and a large stock of chewing-gum. Perhaps they are still there, because I forgot to collect them when we finally went away.

The banyan tree grew behind the house. Its spreading branches, which hung to the ground and took root again, formed a number of twisting passageways which gave me endless pleasure. The tree was older than the house, older than my grandparents, as old as Dehra. I could hide myself in its branches, behind thick green leaves, and spy on the world below. I could read in it, too, propped up against the bole of the tree, with *Treasure Island* or the *Jungle Books* or comics like *Wizard* or *Hotspur* which, unlike the forbidden *Superman* and others like him, were full of clean-cut schoolboy heroes.

The banyan tree was a world in itself, populated with small beasts and large insects. While the leaves were still pink and tender, they would be visited by the delicate Map Butterfly, who committed her eggs to their care. The 'honey' on the leaves—an edible smear—also attracted the little striped squirrels, who soon grew used to my presence and became quite bold. Red-headed parakeets swarmed about the tree early in the mornings.

But the banyan really came to life during the monsoon, when the branches were thick with scarlet figs. These berries were not fit for human consumption, but the many birds that gathered in the tree—gossipy Rosy Pastors, quarrelsome Mynas, cheerful Bulbuls and Coppersmiths, and sometimes a raucous bullying crow—feasted on them. And when night fell, and the birds were resting, the dark Flying Foxes flapped heavily about the tree, chewing and munching as they clambered over the branches.

Among nocturnal visitors to the jackfruit and banyan trees was the Brainfever bird, whose real name is the Hawk-Cuckoo. 'Brainfever, brainfever!' it seems to call, and this shrill, nagging cry will keep the soundest of sleepers awake on a hot summer's night.

The British called it the Brainfever bird, but there are other names for it. The Marathas called it 'Paos-ala,' which means

'Rain is coming!' Perhaps Grandfather's interpretation of its call was the best. According to him, when the bird was tuning up for its main concert, it seemed to say: 'Oh dear, oh dear! How very hot it's getting! We feel it... we feel it... WE FEEL IT!'

Yes, the banyan tree was a noisy place during the rains. If the Brainfever bird made music by night, the crickets and cicadas orchestrated during the day. As musicians, the cicadas were in a class by themselves. All through the hot weather their chorus rang through the garden, while a shower of rain, far from damping their spirits, only roused them to a greater vocal effort.

The tree-crickets were a band of willing artistes who commenced their performance at almost any time of the day but preferably in the evenings. Delicate pale green creatures with transparent green wings, they were hard to find amongst the lush monsoon foliage; but once located, a tap on the leaf or bush on which they sat would put an immediate end to the performance.

At the height of the monsoon, the banyan tree was like an orchestra-pit with the musicians constantly turning up. Birds, insects and squirrels expressed their joy at the end of the hot weather and the cool quenching relief of the rains.

A flute in my hands, I would try adding my shrill piping to theirs. But they thought poorly of my musical ability, for, whenever I played on the flute, the birds and insects would subside into a pained and puzzled silence.

The Trees Are My Brothers

It's good to know that my old friend the jackfruit is finally coming into its own. Apparently it is now much in demand in the West, a fashionable substitute for meat, being used as filling for burgers, sandwiches, pies etc., with one enthusiast even calling it 'mutton hanging from a tree'.

Here in India we have always appreciated a good jackfruit curry, or even better, a jackfruit pickle. I'm a pickle friend myself, and among the twenty different pickles on my sideboard there is always a jar of jackfruit pickle; that's why I call it an old friend. But I had no idea it tasted like mutton. The seed and the pulp have their own individual flavour. As it grows on a tree we call it a fruit, but we cook it as though it were a vegetable. And it, to some, tastes like mutton, then perhaps some meat-eaters will become vegetarians. On the other hand, some vegetarians might not care for its meaty flavour!

When I was a boy, we had an old jackfruit tree growing beside the side veranda. I spent a lot of time in the trees surrounding my grandmother's bungalow, and this one was easy to climb. The others included several guava and lichi trees, lemons and grapefruits, and of course a couple of mango trees—but these last were difficult to climb.

'Why do you spend so much time in the trees?' complained my grandmother. 'Why not do something useful for a change?'

'The trees are my brothers,' I would say, 'I like to play with them.'

And I still think of them as my brothers, although I can no longer climb trees or play in them. But I still think of them as human beings possessed of individuality and charm. Just as no two humans are exactly alike (unless they happen to be twins), so no two trees are the same. Like humans they grow from seed. They develop branches as arms and leaves like flowing hair. We give birth to children, they give birth to fruits and flowers. We shelter our young, they shelter the small creatures of the forest.

However, unlike us, they spring from the soul, from the land—the very land that gives us food and pasture and protection; the land that we so casually take for granted, preferring to build upon it rather than grow upon it. Where will our cattle graze when the last green spaces have gone?

'No problem,' says a young friend. 'We can always import our milk.'

The other day I came across an old book that had been on my shelf for many years. *Farmer's Glory* by A.G. Street, written several decades ago. In his epilogue he writes:

> It is perhaps nothing to boast about, but there is little doubt that the present prosperity of British farming is mainly due to one man, who is now dead. His name was Adolf Hitler. There is no disputing that it was the fear of famine during the early 1940s which taught the British nation that despite all man's cleverness and

Learn
character from
trees,
values from
roots
and change
from
leaves

inventions, when real danger comes an island, people must turn for succour to the only permanent asset they possess, the land of their own country. It has never, and will never, let them down; always provided they realize and obey this eternal truth—that to make the land serve man, man must first be content to serve the land.

Surely it is this love of the land and willingness to serve it that is at the heart of true patriotism. The patriotic songs and speeches that we hear from time to time are fine for stirring up the emotions, but it is really the connect between ourselves and the '*do bigha zameen*' on which we grow our fruit and grain that emboldens us to protect it.

I think I am correct in saying that most of our jawans, the young men who join the solid ranks of the Indian Army, come from rural backgrounds; some from the hills, some from the vast plains and hinterland of our country. They know the value of the land. They have grown up in villages and have worked with their families in the rice fields, or sugar cane plantations, or mango groves, or wheat or corn or mustard or fields of an infinite variety of crops. More than city folk, they know the value of the land—its true worth in terms of either prosperity or poverty. And so they are ready to defend it, to fight for it against all corners. The best soldiers come from the soil that they and their forefathers have tilled.

So let us protect the land—not just from the intruder or the enemy, but also from those who would turn the field or the forest into one more concrete jungle.

Of course there are those who prefer concrete jungles. Like

my young friend who wants to live in a Smart City and never mind the cities that are no longer smart. My advice to him (unheeded of course) is to go back to his roots, create a smart little village, and plant jackfruit trees!

The Sal

The sal loves the company of its friends and family. Extensive stretches of sal forest clothe the Shivalik rages around the Doon valley; but if you plant a single sal tree out on its own, in your garden or in a park, it will be most unhappy, refusing to grow or flourish likes its fellows in the forest.

It is a valuable timber tree, hard and durable, much desired for its use in buildings, railway sleepers, etc., and the forest department very wisely protects its sal forests, from Uttarakhand to Assam and across the Vindhyas to Madhya Pradesh.

According to Buddhist tradition, the Buddha was born and attained Nirvana under the sal tree. In the spring, the sal forests are in full bloom, their flowers emitting a heady fragrance, to the delight of the birds, butterflies and humans.

This is the tree most often mentioned in Kipling's *Jungle Book,* and whenever I pass through a sal forest, I can visualize Mowgli and his friend Bagheera (the black panther) padding silently over the fallen leaves that carpet the forest floor.

Among the Mountain Forests

India is probably nowhere so rich in forests as in the Himalayas, where the hills and valleys provide so many contrasts in elevation, humidity and temperature that a great variety of vegetation is to be found all the year round.

Ascending the foothills, no very sudden change is noticed, and it almost seems that the vast stretch of forest lying in the still heat is merely a duplicate of the forest in the plains. But this is a sal forest, which covers the foothills with speed and persistence. The more vigorous sal trees grow rapidly, the weaker bide their time until the death or destruction of their more powerful fellows.

A sal forest has a remarkably individual character, where, from tiny sapling to giant patriarch, each tree ruthlessly waits for the downfall of its neighbour: a restless, ambitious sea of foliage, some trees attaining a height of 150 feet and a girth of twenty feet.

The sal is the most important tree of the lower Himalayas, providing the bulk of railway sleepers in India and yielding, when tapped, a large quantity of good resin. The flowers, tiny and sweet-scented, appear in March, in some places heralding a spring festival, when baskets of them are carried from village to village and distributed to women as emblems of motherhood.

Beyond the sal forests, the hillside changes in appearance. The undergrowth is not so tall. It thins out, and the only features suggesting tropical vegetation are the giant mops of the screw pine and the beautiful tree ferns.

Now the birch and the poplar prevail. The Himalayan Birches, growing singly, are more valued for their bark than for their timber. The bark is cast off in wide, horizontal shreds, and is exported far and wide for tanning, papermaking and lining of hookahs. The poplar's broad, heart-shaped leaves readily flutter to every breeze; and apart from the tree's ornamental value, its close-grained timber is used for beams and rafters.

In the eastern hills, where the monsoon is heavy, the atmosphere is too humid for the coniferous family, but just suits the immigrant Japanese Cedar, which grows with such persistence that many of these trees, trim and beautiful and straight, are found at elevations of 4,000 to 6,000 feet—elevations which also happen to suit most of the flora of temperate Europe.

The oak and the chestnut grow profusely above 5,000 feet. The fruit of the chestnut is beloved by the Lepchas of Sikkim, and the wood of this tree provides the big pestles and mortars used for crashing millets, which are converted into local beer.

On the more exposed hills grow the maples, trees of no great size or thickness, but of striking appearance in the spring and autumn by the variety of crimson and gold tints in their foliage. There are several species of maple, and the best drinking cups in Tibet are made from the knobs of one particular kind of tree.

The walnut is a native of the eastern Himalayas, and bears a high percentage of good nuts. It is also in great demand for making furniture.

The rhododendrons and magnolias are the most admired trees of the Himalayas. The rhododendron's magnificent cluster of pink and crimson bells explains the meaning of its name—rhododendron, rose tree!

Near Darjeeling in West Bengal, the magnolia has deep wine-coloured flowers, which are very fragrant—so sweet that they have been known to cause giddiness to the inhaler.

The pine, deodar, cedar, yew and spruce are all well-known conifers in the Himalayas. Many beautiful bamboos abound in the hills—one species is used by the Lepchas for making bows, another is used in floating heavy logs and a third, when cut, shortened and flattened out, serves the purpose of tiles; it is durable and watertight.

The peach and the apricot, the plum and the cherry, grow wild and in cultivation, and their delicate pink and white blossoms add charm and grace to the grandeur of the Himalayas.

Storms
make trees
take deeper
roots

The Friendly Banyan

It's the hour of cow dust.
A slanting sunbeam strikes
Through the gathering mist
And turns the dust to gold.
The grazing cattle stream home.
The wading egrets seek shelter,
And in the over-arching banyan tree
The mynas squabble, the squirrels play
The fruit-bats come to life;
And then the sun sinks in the west,
And in the friendly banyan tree there's rest.

I wrote these lines only a few minutes ago. I had only to think of the majestic banyan tree, and I found myself breaking into verse!

As a boy, how I loved to explore the passageways created by the tree's aerial roots—those spreading branches that hung to the ground and created fresh roots. The banyan tree will keep spreading, if you will allow it to do so. But they do need plenty of space—the outskirts of a village, the banks of a pond, the centre of a park. Don't disturb those aerial roots. If you cut them away, this mighty tree might well topple over. Those roots are like the pillars that support a temple.

Gentle Shade by Day

Those who have spent time in non-air-conditioned parts of India will remember with gratitude those gracious trees that provide shade and shelter during the summer months—the banyan, peepul, mango, neem and others. Coastal dwellers are not so fortunate for there is not much shade to be had from a palm tree unless you keep moving in its long but insubstantial shadow.

I am not surprised that the sages of old were given to sitting beneath the peepul tree. They might have had various religious reasons for calling it sacred but I am sure there was a good practical reason as well. Few trees provide a cooler shade than it does. Even on the stillest of days, the peepul leaves are forever twirling and with thousands of leaves spinning like tops, there is quite a breeze for anyone sitting below.

However, there are warnings about peepul trees—'Gentle shade by day and terror by night!' During the night, the tree is said to be alive with various spirits, most of them inimical to man. One is advised not to sleep beneath it, for this is construed by a ghost as an invitation to jump down your throat and take possession of you, or at the very least, ruin your digestion.

It is also said to be unlucky to sleep beneath a tamarind,

but I have often reclined in the pleasant shade of this noble tree and have come to no harm. A famous tamarind stands over the tomb of Tansen, the great musician and singer of Akbar's court at Gwalior. Its leaves, though bitter, are eaten by singers to improve their voices.

A mango grove is a wonderful place for an afternoon siesta. But if the mangoes are ripening, there is usually a great deal of activity going on with parrots, crows, monkeys and small boys, all attempting to evade the watchman who uses an empty kerosene tin as a drum to try and frighten them away. So it's not the ideal place for a nap then, but the shade under a mango grove is dark, deep and very soothing.

The banyan tree with its aerial roots represents the matted hair of Lord Shiva. There is always shade and space beneath a venerable old banyan. It is still a popular community centre in our Indian villages but is becoming a rarity in cities simply because it covers so large an area. And if you cut its aerial roots, the tree topples over. Other handsome trees related to the banyan are the pilkhan and the chilkhan, large spreading evergreens, both quite noticeable on some of New Delhi's wider avenues.

The neem is a tall tree, but its numerous branches give it a shady head. One of my greatest pleasures is to walk beneath an avenue of neem trees after a shower of rain. As the fallen berries are crushed underfoot, they give out a sharp heady fragrance, which I find exhilarating. Apart from its medicinal uses, the tree is connected in legends with the Sun God, as in the story of *Neembarak*. 'The Sun in a Neem Tree', who invited to dinner a Bairagi tribal, whose rules forbade him to eat anything except by daylight. When dinner was delayed after sundown, Suraj

Narayan, the Sun God, obligingly descended from a neem tree and continued shining till dinner was over.

On this pleasant note I end this tribute, only adding that shade-giving trees symbolize the harmony between man and nature and that our ancestors in their devotion to trees and reverence for them, clearly showed that they knew what was good for them.

the best
time to plant
a tree is
20 years ago.
The second
best is now

Under the Deodars

The names of trees often find their way into the titles of books and stories. Kipling's earliest stories were published in India under the title *Under the Deodars*—for it was under the deodars of Shimla that all the scandals, intrigues, romances and hauntings took place!

As you ascend the Himalayan foothills, the trees of the plains give way to the trees of the mountains, and at 7,000 ft. you will be welcomed by the deodars (*Cedrus Deodara*), singly or in large numbers, for these great trees are indigenous to the Himalayas. In the presence of deodars, the air is purer, more bracing. They will give you a sense of renewal.

Deodar, comes from 'devdar', Sanskrit for 'Tree of God'. And indeed no tree could be nobler, growing to a great height and living for two or three hundred years, sometimes longer. Some of the oldest and most magnificent specimens are found in the premises of temples, where they are protected. These great trees are, at their most luxuriant, around 8,000 ft.

A similar tree is the cedar of Lebanon, which grows on the mountains of Lebanon and Syria. Some are reputed to be about 2,000 years old with a girth of some 40 ft. Legend has it that it provided the timber used by King Solomon for building his temple.

Mr V.P. Mehta tells me that at the Forest Research Institute in Dehradun, a cross section of an old deodar shows 700 distinct annual growth rings. The tree was born some time during the reign of Alauddin Khilji in the 12th century, and lived through the Mughal period and the great part of the British rule in India.

If only trees could talk, what great historians they would be!

Death of the Trees

The peace and quiet of the Maplewood hillside disappeared forever one winter. The powers-that-be decided to build another new road into the mountains and the PWD saw fit to take it right past the cottage, about six feet from the window that overlooked the forest.

In my journal I wrote—Already they have felled most of the trees. The walnut was one of the first to go. A tree I had lived with for over ten years, watching it grow as I had watched Prem's small son Rakesh grow up, looking forward to its new leaf-buds, the broad green leaves or summer turning to spears of gold in September when the walnuts were ripe and ready to fall. I knew this tree better than the others. It was just below the window where a buttress for the road was going up.

Another tree I will miss is the young deodar, the only one growing in this stretch of the woods. Some years back it was stunted from lack of sunlight. The oaks covered it with their shaggy branches, so I cut away some of the overhanging ones and after that the deodar grew much faster. It was just coming into its own this year—now cut down in its prime like my young brother on the road to Delhi last month. Both victims of the roads—the tree kilted by the PWD, my brother by a truck.

Twenty oaks have been felled just in this small stretch near the cottage. By the time this bypass reaches Jabai khet, about six miles from here, over a thousand oaks will have been slaughtered, besides many other fine trees—maples, deodars and pines—most of them unnecessarily as they grew some fifty or sixty yards from the roadside.

The trouble is, hardly anyone (with the exception of the contractor who buys the felled trees) really believes that trees and shrubs are necessary. They get in the way so much, don't they? According to my milkman, the only useful tree is the one that can be picked clean of its leaves for fodder! And a young man remarked to me, 'You should come to Pauri. The view is terrific, there's not a tree in the way!'

Well he can stay here now and enjoy the view of the ravaged hillside. But as the oaks have gone, the milkman will have to look further afield for his fodder.

Rakesh calls the maples butterfly trees because when the winged seeds fall, they flutter like butterflies in the breeze. No maples now. No bright red leaves to flame against the sky. No birds! That is to say, no birds near the house. No longer will it be possible for me to open the window and watch the scarlet minivets flitting through the dark green foliage of the oaks... the long-tailed magpies gliding through the trees, the barbet calling insistently from his perch on the top of the deodar. Forest birds, all of them, they will now be in search of some other stretch of surviving forest. The only visitors will be the crows who have learnt to live with and off humans and seem to multiply along with roads, houses and people. And even when all the people have gone, the crows will still be there.

Other things to look forward to—trucks thundering past in the night, perhaps a tea and pakora shop around the corner. The grinding of gears, the music of motor horns. Will the whistling thrush be heard above them? The explosions that continually shatter the silence of the mountains as thousand-year-old rocks are dynamited have frightened away all but the most intrepid of birds and animals. Even the bold langurs haven't shown their faces for over a fortnight.

Somehow, I don't think we shall wait for the tea shop to arrive. There must be some other quiet corner, possibly on the next mountain where new roads have yet to come into being. No doubt this is a negative attitude and if I had any sense I'd open my own tea shop. To retreat is to be a loser. But the trees are losers too and when they fall, they do so with a certain dignity.

Never mind. Men come and go, the mountains remain.

The Cherry Tree

One day, when Rakesh was six, he walked home from the Mussoorie bazaar eating cherries. They were a little sweet, a little sour; small, bright red cherries that had come all the way from the Kashmir Valley.

Here in the Himalayan foothills where Rakesh lived, there were not many fruit trees. The soil was stony, and the dry cold winds stunted the growth of most plants. But on the more sheltered slopes there were forests of oak and deodar.

Rakesh lived with his grandfather on the outskirts of Mussoorie, just where the forest began. His father and mother lived in a small village fifty miles away, where they grew maize and rice and barley in narrow terraced fields on the lower slopes of the mountain. But there were no schools in the village, and Rakesh's parents were keen that he should go to school. As soon as he was of school-going age, they sent him to stay with his grandfather in Mussoorie.

Grandfather was a retired forest ranger. He had a little cottage outside the town.

Rakesh was on his way home from school when he bought the cherries. He paid fifty paise for the bunch. It took him about half an hour to walk home, and by the time he reached the cottage there were only three cherries left.

'Have a cherry, Grandfather,' he said, as soon as he saw his grandfather in the garden.

Grandfather took one cherry and Rakesh promptly ate the other two. He kept the last seed in this mouth for some time, rolling it round and round on his tongue until all the tang had gone. Then he placed the seed on the palm of his hand and studied it.

'Are cherry seeds lucky?' asked Rakesh.

'Of course.'

'Then I'll keep it.'

'Nothing is lucky if you put it away. If you want luck, you must put it to some use.'

'What can I do with a seed?'

'Plant it.'

So Rakesh found a small shade and began to dig up a flower bed.

'Hey, not there,' said Grandfather. 'I've sown mustard in that bed. Plant it in that shady corner where it won't be disturbed.'

Rakesh went to a corner of the garden where the earth was soft and yielding. He did not have to dig. He pressed the seed into the soil with his thumb and it went right in.

Then he had his lunch and ran off to play cricket with his friends and forgot all about the cherry seed.

When it was winter in the hills, a cold wind blew down from the snows and went *whoo-whoo-whoo* through the deodar trees, and the garden was dry and bare. In the evenings, Grandfather told Rakesh stories—stories about people who turned into animals, and ghosts who lived in trees, and beans that jumped and stones that wept—and in turn Rakesh would read to him from the newspaper, Grandfather's eyesight being rather weak. Rakesh found the newspaper very dull—especially after the stories—but Grandfather wanted all the news...

They knew it was spring when the wild duck flew north again, to Siberia. Early in the morning, when he got up to chop wood and light a fire, Rakesh saw the V-shaped formation streaming northwards, the calls of the birds carrying clearly through the thin mountain air.

One morning in the garden, he bent to pick up what he thought was a small twig and found to his surprise that it was well-rooted. He stared at it for a moment, then ran to fetch Grandfather, calling, 'Dada, come and look, the cherry tree has come up!'

'What cherry tree?' asked Grandfather, who had forgotten about it.

'The seed we planted last year—look, it's come up!'

Rakesh went down on his haunches, while Grandfather bent almost double and peered down at the tiny tree. It was about four inches high.

'Yes, it's a cherry tree,' said Grandfather. 'You should water it now and then.'

Rakesh ran indoors and came back with a bucket of water.

'Don't drown it!' said Grandfather.

Rakesh gave it a sprinkling and circled it with pebbles.

'What are the pebbles for?' asked Grandfather.

'For privacy,' said Rakesh.

He looked at the tree every morning but it did not seem to be growing very fast. So, he stopped looking at it—except quickly, out of the corner of his eye. And, after a week or two, when he allowed himself to look at it properly, he found that it had grown—at least an inch!

That year the monsoon rains came early and Rakesh plodded to and from school in raincoat and gum boots. Ferns sprang from the trunks of trees, strange-looking lilies came up in the long grass, and even when it wasn't raining the trees dripped, and mist came curling up the valley. The cherry tree grew quickly in this season.

It was about two feet high when a goat entered the garden and ate all the leaves. Only the main stem and two thin branches remained.

'Never mind,' said Grandfather, seeing that Rakesh was upset. 'It will grow again, cherry trees are tough.'

Towards the end of the rainy season new leaves appeared on the tree. Then a woman cutting grass scrambled down the hillside, her scythe swishing through the heavy monsoon foliage. She did not try to avoid the tree: one sweep, and the cherry tree was cut in two.

When Grandfather saw what had happened, he went after the woman and scolded her; but the damage could not be repaired.

'Maybe it will die now,' said Rakesh.

'Maybe,' said Grandfather.

But the cherry tree had no intention of dying.

By the time summer came round again, it had sent out several new shoots with tender green leaves. Rakesh had grown taller too. He was eight now, a sturdy boy with curly black hair and deep black eyes. Blackberry eyes, Grandfather called them.

That monsoon Rakesh went home to his village, to help his father and mother with the planting and ploughing and sowing. He was thinner but stronger when he came back to Grandfather's house at the end of the rains, to find that the cherry tree had grown another foot. It was now up to his chest.

Even when there was rain, Rakesh would sometimes water the tree. He wanted it to know that he was there.

One day he found a bright green praying mantis perched on a branch, peering at him with bulging eyes. Rakesh let it remain there. It was the cherry tree's first visitor.

The next visitor was a hairy caterpillar, who started making a meal of the leaves. Rakesh removed it quickly and dropped it on a heap of dry leaves.

'They're pretty leaves,' said Rakesh. 'And they are always ready to dance. If there's a breeze.'

After Grandfather had come indoors, Rakesh went into the garden and lay down on the grass beneath the tree. He gazed up through the leaves at the great blue sky; and turning on his side, he could see the mountain striding away into the clouds. He was still lying beneath the tree when the evening shadows crept across the garden. Grandfather came back and sat down beside Rakesh, and they waited in silence until the stars came out and the nightjar began to call. In the forest below, the crickets and cicadas began tuning up; and suddenly the tree was full of the sound of insects.

'There are so many trees in the forest,' said Rakesh. 'What's so special about this tree? Why do we like it so much?'

'We planted it ourselves,' said Grandfather. 'That's why it's special.'

'Just one small seed,' said Rakesh, and he touched the smooth bark of the tree that had grown. He ran his hand along the trunk of the tree and put his finger to the tip of a leaf. 'I wonder,' he whispered, 'is this what it feels like to be God?'

Ruba - 1274
19/5/22